Beyond The Burning Shore

Ron Foster
Alabama, USA

ISBN-13:
978-1541381964

ISBN-10:
1541381963

Printed in the United States of America.

Acknowledgements

Sea Eagle Boats, Inc.

Power Film Solar

RELiON Batteries

TNW Firearms

O.F. Mossberg & Sons

Daiwa

Panther Martin

Tangled Tales of An American Family

Heracane Anne

1

What If the Biggest Solar Storm on Record Happened Tomorrow?

Hogan stared out through the window shades of his Atlanta apartment craning his neck to look towards the river and wondering if it would be a good day for fishing tomorrow. He had been diligently watching and researching space weather reports on the internet for the last week for many reasons. One of the reasons was his latest scientific and personal curiosity if geomagnetic storms affected game fishes predatory instincts.

Some folks might say upon meeting him for the first time that this odd character seemed to be unusually fixated on the subject of solar storms. The reasoning behind this observation was because he often brought the celestial phenomenon up during conversations at the local watering hole that he liked to frequent after work sometimes.

He would knowingly tell his bar patron friends as well as strangers that got within conversation distance of him on many occasions "Static on TV, a solar storm was causing it, phone not working... a solar storm was the problem, he would even advise tourists that they shouldn't travel on a specific day because of the geomagnetic storms that were supposed to be occurring on a certain date increased the radiation they would be exposed to in the airplanes cabin.

No conversation was ever complete or totally over in Hogan's mind unless he had managed to mention somewhere in it a few of his explanations and thoughts about the great Solar Storm of 1859 known as the Carrington Event.

He seemed to particularly enjoy talking about how that famous solar storm had managed to set fire to telegraph offices and wooden buildings worldwide back then and what did people think would happen today if a mega solar flare occurred again with our dependence on technology.

Most people had never heard of or for that matter even considered the possibility of this type of disaster reeking havoc upon modern technology before. Hogan delighted in entertaining his questioners and skeptical listeners with his historic knowledge and rhetoric of what had occurred on that historic eventful day. He also had a few warnings and survival tips for those that asked or would listen to his advisements.

The first thing that he had to do was get them to wrap their heads around just exactly what a solar storm was and wasn't. Mostly all he wanted them to realize was that this type of space weather storm occurs all the time and that they weren't some weird once in a lifetime historical fluke of note like the dinosaurs dying off from an asteroid.

Pretty much everyone seemed to have already heard of the Northern Lights or Auroras that occur regularly lighting up the sky in the Northwest. As the magnetosphere gets bombarded by solar winds, stunning blue lights can appear over the upper reaches of the Northern hemisphere and the lower parts of the southern hemisphere.

Many people knew about this phenomenon but most people don't know the magnitude of destruction of the 1859 super solar storm. They didn't know for example that it has been documented that the solar flares of that particular storm were so powerful that "people in the northeastern U.S. could read newspaper print just from the light of the aurora that night. He liked to detail how the telegraph operators of those times got electrically shocked and how telegraph systems all over Europe and North America had failed and sprayed out fiery sparks from telegraph poles that ignited widespread fires.

Inevitably the subject would turn to modern times and he was asked "What was it he thought" professionally would happen in this technology jazzed up cell phone reliant world we lived in.

"It is going to be like living in pure hell!" He would say with a warning sigh. "Not if, but when we experienced a repeat of the 1859 Carrington Event it would devastate the modern world and send humanity back technology-wise to the 1800's. It was only recently that NASA just observed and recorded a non earth facing coronal mass ejection that was about double the size of the 1859 one which is very scary indeed. The scientists didn't know until recently that those storms can go off the charts in power when trying to be measured with the instruments we had. " Hogan would say with a serious look on his face

Hogan would then go down the list of infrastructure failures a solar storm would cause like no gas, no ATMs, no street lights, no traffic signals, no cell phones etc. He would go on and on elaborating that compared to that event, today's information superhighway, the telegraph system in 1859 may have appeared to be nothing more than a mere foot path or dirt road, but the "Victorian Internet" as it were was also a critical means of transmitting news, sending private messages and engaging in commerce. He mentioned lots of stuff people didn't really want to know at first like our current fragile system of just in time grocery deliveries being affected by no gas for the trucks to deliver. But they got more concerned and interested in the subject as the night grew longer and after he added some recent history.

Just a little bit of space weather interference can cause havoc like when the entire Province of Quebec Canada in 1989 went dark. When that particular solar storm started up the solar flare that accompanied the suns outburst immediately caused short-wave radio interference, including the jamming of radio signals from Radio Free Europe into Russia. It was thought that the signals had been jammed by the Kremlin, but it was only the sun acting up!

Then In less than 2 minutes whoosh, the entire Quebec power grid lost power. During the 12-hour blackout that followed, millions of people suddenly found themselves in dark office buildings and underground pedestrian tunnels, and some experienced the panic of being trapped in stalled elevators. Most people woke up to icy cold homes for breakfast. The blackout also closed schools and businesses; it also kept the Montreal Metro shut during the morning rush hour, and closed Dorval Airport stranding travelers.

What If the Biggest Solar Storm on Record Happened Tomorrow?

Now keep in mind the Quebec Blackout was by no means a local event although you can get geographic based storms. Some of the U.S. electrical utilities had their own cliffhanger problems to deal with. New York Power lost 150 megawatts the moment the Quebec power grid went down. The New England Power Pool lost 1,410 megawatts at about the same time. Service to 96 electrical utilities in New England was interrupted while other reserves of electrical power were brought online. Luckily, the U.S. had the power to spare at the time...but just barely. Across the United States from coast to coast, over 200 power grid problems erupted within minutes of the start of the March 13 storm. Fortunately, none of these caused a blackout. But Hogan warned "It could all happen again... in the blink of an eye an event could cause grid down societal destruction." That's what he worried about, that's what he tried to plan for.

This was usually when the conversation went one way or the other and for better or worse. When he was asked what it was he thought about whatever it was the government was doing about avoiding the geomagnetic mega disaster he was predicting. Hogan explained it wasn't a personal doomsday prophecy of his but that NASA said a CME of magnitude that could destroy infrastructure had a 10-12 % chance of happening at any given moment. It wasn't an "if" but a "when" scenario. His reply as to what the Government was going to do emergency management wise when one actually did happen stunned and flabbergasted them no end. The fact was that the Government was basically doing nothing more than talking about it. Talk! That's all they have done for years is talk about it and the power companies lobby that the safety measures are too expensive for the anticipated risk.

This is the particular point when the big change in conversation generally came about after Hogan admitted to being a prepper and enjoyed being part of that survival minded community. (Someone who prepares for disasters is called a prepper) He prepared for solar storms and grid down situations. He watched their faces carefully for their reactions whether positive or negative to this you would think a non politically correct statement by the reactions of some people.

Generally, a tense laugh off response was necessary and an explanation that no, he didn't have a bunker to go to followed by another explanation by him that he wasn't one of them crazy "Doomsday Preppers" like you see on NATGEO. Seems a lot of people either don't know what a prepper is or held a media influenced low opinion of all preppers as nut jobs in general.

Some people however occasionally became more friendly and interested in what it took to be a prepper and a lively conversation was struck up. Many people could be heard to remark how sensible that outlook sounded in general especially in these trying times of world and climatic unrest. People also usually agreed with him that their grandparents all had big pantries so what was wrong with going back to living that way and storing some food for hard times and bad weather? People just didn't seem to do that much these days and the majority weren't even ready for something like a snow storm food wise, oftentimes.

Hogan made sure to point out the fact that he was a Business Continuity professional first and foremost though as his job and vocation and that was what had brought him here to Atlanta. Being a practicing prepper as his hobby was secondary to his crisis communication and risk planning in outlooks and outcomes for his clients trying to make their factories and such more resilient to disaster.

He explained that he wrote professional continuity plans for businesses to help try to recover their operations as soon as possible after disasters. This was his livelihood and he pointed out that it was in this bar right here that he had picked up his latest big emergency planning contract.

Being in this business of disaster planning gave him and his clients a rather unique perspective on the effects of solar storms and electromagnetic pulses in general and the big insurance companies had even gotten involved and issued their own findings on financial risk estimated at 2.6 trillion dollars but Hogan didn't know how they came up with that figure.

Maybe a favorite client of his who was sort of a real-estate mogul in this city would wander in and add to the conversation while they were talking he explained, but it was doubtful. The more posh restaurants and country clubs were usually his thing. However his employer followed the insurance market and had some insights.

Anyway, about six months ago, Hogan had been attending an annual symposium for Emergency Planners and had stopped in here for a drink one day when he got to talking to someone just like he was doing now. He had found out the guy owned as well as managed a lot of commercial properties and office buildings. To make a long story short, after a few meetings he had finally convinced the gentleman to buy what he called his ultimate business continuity planning package to include something special added on which the guy had first looked at him somewhat askance about.

Mr. Salsec had been pretty doubtful at first about that special addendum Hogan had added on to the plan he was going to develop and Salsec was concerned that maybe he was going to be possibly scammed in some way by agreeing to purchase it.

Hogan had mentioned that he had had coined the unusual term Space Weather Preparedness Planning as the title for this star wars thing addendum that he was trying to describe. This addendum would be something special above and beyond his normal all inclusive catastrophic planning package. He had even offered quite a discounted deal on the indices to Mr. Salsec but his client took some considerable convincing of its merits before it was accepted in full.

It didn't help matters any at all when Hogan was forced to sheepishly explain to him that he actually had no previous written examples of a Space Weather Preparedness plan to show the man. He had many regular plans from his many vested clients and completed high level licensing courses but none inclusive of space weather.

Hogan finally explained to Mr. Salsec that to his knowledge none of the other Business continuity professionals he was acquainted with had ever written one either, let alone ever even conceived of the notion of just how to approach the subject.

Hogan had hooked Mr. Salsec finally on the idea after he had carefully explained that in his less than humble opinion, that he was the most qualified preparedness expert to do a good job on creating such a plan because he understood prepper mentality and homesteading technology and those facts had perked up the man's interest.

It seems that his new client already had himself a bit of a survivalist bent going on for himself already way before they had met. Mr. Salsec had already taken many of his own practical precautions in order to insure his families survival grid down from any number of catastrophic events like a cyber attack, terrorist attack, dirty bomb, a tornado swarm etc. but he hadn't given a whole lot of thought to space weather just yet. He had not also for that matter considered just what plain long-term power outages completely shutting down his businesses could do.

What do you do with businesses that are forced to shut down for extended periods of time so that one day they can maybe reopen and return to profitability? Are there possibly any opportunities that can be taken advantage of during the rebuilding or response phases etc in the aftermath of such a calamity to benefit or profit from?

Hogan really had to sit himself down and do a lot of deep soul searching to firmly decide to vacate his home and take on this particular job. The main point of contention for him in accepting this new position meant that he would have to move from rural Alabama to the big city of Atlanta for a period of at least nine or ten long months.

This move was necessary primarily due to his new workload of having to be onsite to safety overview a lot of properties as well as personally inspect a whole lot of trucking supply roads and personnel highway escape routes. A job like this had a lot for him to consider and evaluate and he had seriously considered hiring and taking on some extra help to accomplish it.

The owner and president of the company that he had contracted with had offered as part of Hogan's compensation to let him stay in a furnished rental property for the duration of the job rent free as well as give him per diem for meals. This sounded pretty good to Hogan at first, he thought he might possibly be in hog heaven on this job until considering what exactly the offer entailed.

Securing this contract would give him a chance to save up some money and also possibly expand his small business. However, he wasn't very happy with the accommodations. The offered lodging was in an upscale, dead in the middle of downtown high rise apartment complex and there was no way in hell he was staying in a place that was reliant on an elevator or had not one tree in sight.

After a bit of dickering on his part and a considerable amount whining about why he needed a little bit of open space that contained some green vegetation or a tree in it once in awhile, he finally got himself installed cost free in a nice common working man's apartment in an adjoining town next to the Chattahoochee River called Roswell.

He hadn't told his boss about his paranoia of all things that had more than five floors or anything taller than a Fire departments hook and ladder truck's reach so he was picky as to what was acceptable. Force of habit and his own personal safety measures and tastes as well as his love of just plain space consisting of grass and trees influenced his decision.

He normally lived in a small house in the middle of five wooded acres that had a little garden and a tiny creek. He didn't give two hoots at all that he just had turned down a pretty much free prestigious $5,000 a month apartment for a common one that rented for $850.00. He had his reasons; he also had his personal sanity to think about. To him the apartment he had found was perfect and it was away from downtown and living that close to the river sounded like fun.

Reason number one on that he had located where he did was that he had already figured out using his prepper sense just how close it was that he wanted to be to an aqueous door out of this city should a devastating fire occur. However, beyond that he had already started figuring out which road was the best way for him and his van to get out of this place fast come SHTF for a variety of nasty reasons that ranged from terrorist dirty bomb to a cyber attack destroying a satellite, etc.

People could call him paranoid or say he had become preparedness balmy from doing that odd job of his if they wanted too, but he had the chance to pre-position himself in this move and he was going to do it practical and tactical.

He had decided that his housing search started on the fringes of the city proper and must be near a water feature, a short commute to work as his number one priority to look for.

Mr. Salsec or "Boss" as Hogan often referred to him amicably, using the boss title as a nickname was indeed his boss in many ways. Although you had to understand theirs was a strictly contractual agreement association and not an employer-employee relationship.

Frank Salsec didn't seem to get this strict division of freedoms at times though and they had their few small differences but not very often. This stubbornness on Mr. Salsec's part was probably due to his affluence and age usually holding sway over Hogan's objections, who in turn rarely had to remind Mr. Salsec he was an independent contractor and did things in his own way and on his own time schedule, but that's another story.

What If the Biggest Solar Storm on Record Happened Tomorrow?

Mostly in the beginning of their association, Mr. Salsec began expanding his preparedness learning from Hogan about the more obscure threats existing in the world in general and to his company specifically.

Hogan's planning was well received and sufficient for that task however over time Mr. Salsec shifted the focus eventually to preparing more for his family specifically and distracting Hogan.

Hogan didn't mind telling him survival tips and tricks over lunch or long drinking bouts at this little pub about what was necessary prepperwise to take care of his family, but he couldn't write a business plan like that for a company. Well he could, but he wasn't about to make it his life's work to hang out and provide preparedness advice at that level to every employee or manager the guy had.

Hogan explained that much of this general kind of preparedness information needed was freely available on the internet and if more was needed for the employees' basic preparedness, brochures were available for cost or no cost from the government printing office.

Many continuity planners as well as the would be so called preparedness consultants just add that free stuff to their plan and charged for it, but Hogan wasn't one to do that. This kind of "See Spot Run" Dick and Mary Jane level of preparedness examples for the uninitiated was not something he was willing to get into. That kind of FEMA awareness or resilient community information was a necessity but something that a big corporation like Mr. Salsec's safety officer should have already addressed, Hogan had explained

Boss asked Hogan if he would consider sticking around a bit longer in his duties if he himself put a word in with the Country Club for them to hire him to write their continuity plan.

"Why is that?" Hogan had asked.

"Because you could get a major contract and I could make a bunch of money on the side and we would both feel better about ourselves." Boss said with a broad grin.

"Ha boss! I would feel a little bit better if you had started that conversation out with that I could make a bunch of money and that you could get a major contract that YOU needed to take care of instead of me. I am stretched pretty thin time wise with my work already. What did you do? Go and start talking to all those business men about continuity plans? Were you sitting with those the country club ones you were telling me about that only have their IT divisions Disaster operation plans that may or may not include backing up their servers in another state written down somewhere if needed?" Hogan asked remembering he had been asked if he could recommend anyone in that particular field because Hogan didn't do the technical electronic aspects of disaster planning. He usually just reviewed the techs plans and then added the human elements they never contained like the phone numbers for all employees on a pass around sheet, a way to disseminate news to employees regarding wages etc, what to do in a quarantine environment if it was declared etc.

"Yea I did go do something like that, what did you tell me you called it when you sucked me into paying for all this preparedness planning? Your 4 foot effect I think it was that you called it where everyone within 4 feet of you knew what business you were in and you engaged the first interested person that looked like they had money that spoke to you? See, I do listen to you Hogan!" The boss said catching Hogan off guard about how much information he just gave away about himself every time they met.

'Well yes I do admit that with you I sort of got pointed in your direction as a lead to solicit some business from because someone pointed you out. But I do ok on my own that way, I love to network. I started doing that solicitation crap when I tried my hand at being a stockbroker back in the day; only thing worse is an insurance salesman. I guess until I think of a wily old real-estate wheeler dealer like you sniffing around for a victim. I already told you I would put my name, titles and recommendations on the Business Continuity Company you proposed. That was mostly based on if I could look over other professionals' plans and make suggestions. But if you remember right I told you city living wasn't for me and I could do most of the work from my home office in the sticks." Hogan said proud as a peacock he was asked to head up such a firm with the power of Salsec money and influence but loving his country boy freedoms more.

"Well, hear me out Hogan, before we go to the ballroom at the Country Club for a meeting I would appreciate you visiting my barber, you are starting to look like Samson." Boss said getting an immediate eye clinch and a bite your tongue held back retort to the insult to Hogan's alleged dignity.

"Now you just go right ahead and get your feathers unruffled Hogan. You know I didn't mean to offend you none. Nothing wrong with you getting yourself spiffed up once in awhile. I bet you clean up good! If you remember, I told you awhile back that I was going to take a poke at you and hurt your feelings in business occasionally. I do that to make you uncomfortable sometimes to see how you act under pressure, hell boy if I am paying you top dollar to deal with how my employees are supposed to act in hard times, I better see you doing the same in the real world as well as the apocalyptic scenarios you scare the crap out of me every day with. Now before you turn me down flat on my proposition hear me out. I tell you what, you might know how to camp out in the woods better than me under adverse conditions but I know business better than you ever will. Look here, I don't need to even ask someone to seriously consider giving you the Atlanta Country Club contract to increase your business and prestige. All I got to do is ask a favor and get it printed in the newspaper that you are possibly being considered for the job and you can make more money than you can think of making using that headline as a reference! Now hush up and let's get to the meat of the matter as your country butt is always telling me." Boss said huffily losing patience with Hogan's either put on or actual country way of southern negotiations when he wanted out of something.

"Ok my friend I am in, I will even get me a real fancy haircut for you. What's on your mind that's so all fired important it's got to be that day?" Hogan said looking for the bar maid.

"I don't care about your hair you know that, just get it styled a might because you are going to be playing Hollywood and making appearances to the rich and famous as it were. I got to thinking about all them articles you send me sometimes of the super rich building bunkers and such for themselves and others at the community level and they got me to thinking about a new real estate angle. That country club owns a large acreage on the bend of that river, they already jacked the prices for folks having golf course homes etc and of course they got their little conclave thing going. A whole lot of retirees live there, they pay lots of extra cash for security, landscaping, home owners association fees etc. so I said why not add disaster preparedness to that mix? Seems to me you already know everybody and their brother in the manufacturing end or suppliers to the prepper community for food and gear. If you got a membership there and moved around and mingled a little as well as do the emergency plan for that area you could make a million bucks maybe." Boss offered reminding Hogan it wasn't what you know in life, but who you know oftentimes that makes you successful.

"Aw man now you got me intrigued and maybe just a bit greedy!" Hogan said slurping his drink before catching himself and responding negatively.

"Frank that would work, I know it would probably work like gangbusters but I can't do it. If I don't believe in the product you better believe I can't sell it and what's worse than that is if somebody has just got money to burn I can suggest something preparedness wise until the sun comes up something to buy. But as I told you just having survival stuff is worthless if they have the wrong mindset. Tell you what, I can show you some plans that Japanese Emergency Management is using right now for stocking community warehouses of supplies and you can mimic that. I am not into retailing how expensive of a bug out bag to sell folks the components of with a straight face. I usually tell people most of what they buy is too much or unnecessary." Hogan objected.

"I ain't talking about us getting into that kind of business at all. I know you got ideals and won't just sell crap to make a nickel. You are the one that has been preaching all that prepper homesteader rhetoric at me and I understand the reason you want to go back to your little house in the country away from this big city. Tell you what, you put your emergency manager hat back on and get them rich folks to follow you down the same path you follow as a prepper and it might get your preparedness message to go mainstream better." Boss said before adding "wasn't it Hogan who had said the government spent millions every year trying to get the hurricane prone gulf coast residents to put together a 72 hour kit but only 40% ever did it? This was his chance to try to do the same thing but now he could do it Hogan's cheaper, better way."

"Yes, I remember telling you that. It wasn't until they nearly doubled the amount of dollars spent and started everyone on an advertising campaign of preparing for the mythical "zombie apocalypse" that they got better results." Hogan answered

Hogan hated that particular media campaign. It gave the excuse for snot-nosed kids and adults alike to ask their parents to buy big ass knives, swords and axes and such they had no business with without understanding it wasn't a silly role-playing game. But Mr. Salsec was right; getting the preparedness message out was a driving force in Hogan's life so he listened patiently.

"Now back to the country club, you can look at apartment rentals and investment returns the closer you are to that amenity being higher than places like where you are living now. What if when you paid your deposit down on an apartment and you were guaranteed by a corporation food and preparations being provided for a disaster located in one of those little Japanese shipping container things we talked about along with a renter's insurance policy? See you got age restrictive retirement communities etc that have certain caveats in their leasing how about established preparedness communities?" Boss said letting the idea sink in.

"Pretty cool, an already pre-made resilient community setup, why not?" If he could have moved into one for an affordable extra fee he would have done it himself." Hogan considered.

"I take it you been maybe looking around buying property options?" Hogan said wryly with a small smirk in boss's direction as he eyed the bar to see if anyone appeared to be listening too closely to them talking business.

"Of course I have considered doing it but that's none of your business right now, the idea is would you consider writing the Country Clubs emergency plan and giving a talk to a couple developers I have coming there?" Boss said scrutinizing Hogan's mixed emotions that were furrowing his brow.

Hogan looked up at him and then lowered his head studying his drink that all of the sudden tasted flat. Mr. Salsec wanted answers and he didn't have them. Going to Atlanta wasn't as bad as going to hell in New York City but it felt about the same to him right now as he considered what an extended even longer stay in the big city would mean. No planting spring gardens, no homegrown vegetable harvest, no watching flowers form on the fruit trees in the orchard, no pissing or making a campfire in the backyard or letting loose with his 22 or AR rifle whenever he wanted to, no neighbors dogs coming to visit when they wanted to say hi to him and his mate, no nothing but a big old pile of money if he could forgo such of life's luxuries a little while longer.

"Now as for shaking hands on it and committing to writing a continuity plan you can take a few days to consider. But as for just going to talk about help sell the business and idea of it, I need your answer now." Boss said.

"I told you before that you need a face man for them folks to look at and not me. I can feed whoever it is you find what they need to be concentrating on. Grab another business continuity specialist or emergency manager to tag along that I can direct the grunt work to. That way you got somebody to answer phones and handle objections and I don't find myself backed into a corner trying to handle too much." Hogan suggested.

"We haven't got the time to go interview and hire one. The meeting I am calling is in only a few days. Don't you have a prepper friend around here somewhere that already knows basic human survival needs you can get to tag along with you? Maybe somebody that talks about stocking pantries and camping and canning and such? Don't bring one of them fortress minded or over the top bristling with weapons gun prepper folks though. I would want you to choose someone that can talk about surviving hard times more calmly and holistically, like you do." Boss asked.

"Uh yea, I might be able to come up with someone that would fit the bill and be willing to play the game with me. Is there anything in it for them personally that I can offer as bait or a bonus to get them to go?" Hogan asked thinking about compensation for what might be viewed as a paid acting or reacting job.

"Hell, they get a fine dinner, a bar tab and a hundred bucks for hanging out talking about prepping, is that fair?" Boss asked not having considered this factor yet but thinking Hogan and whoever he brought with him would probably cost $400 bucks in receipts and tips in there if they hit the bar after an expensive dinner for any lengthy time period.

"Sure I will do it, I am not sure who exactly it is yet I am going to drag along with me though. When did you want us to do that thing again?" Hogan asked.

"I know it's short notice but would Wednesday be too early to finalize the meeting date on?" Boss asked flinching when Hogan's eyes momentarily flashed his anger at the time schedule.

"I don't know who I might end up with to help me on such short notice. I will have to think on that. That's ok I can come alone if I have to and we sort it out later. What's that recreational creator or whatever you call that lady that coordinates your employee events think of my Boy Scout idea?" Hogan asked watching the Boss get uncomfortable about one of Hogan's odder suggestions of using the company's non profit paid volunteer works time to focus on preparedness.

A lot of companies these days required their workers to take a week or two weeks off to advance the social model while interacting in things like building houses for Habitat for Humanity or Care Givers Day Off, etc. and doing a bit of community service. Usually the employees were free to choose what they wanted to do but helping a Scout with a preparedness badge or learning something about survival benefited both and Hogan pushed it as an option to get people up to speed quicker to just basically take care of themselves or get out in the outdoors.

Well we got the typical Girls Scouts versus the Boy Scout participations objections but that is the only thing going on which is easily remedied. But the message to do these sorts of things got confused when you started making it sound like play day and including fishing, kayaking and canoeing, reptile study and such. I can easily imagine it will work though all people have to think about is no food, nothing to drink and wishing they had some scouting skills. That's why I wanted you to try to include in your planning some kind of personal level for the employees but I understand it's too difficult right now at this stage." Boss said checking his watch before informing Hogan he had to leave soon.

Well at the personal preparedness level it becomes an individual thing with different needs. There is precedence though; there are Emergency Assistance Funds (EAFs) for Employee Hardship and Disaster Relief. Say for example, there is a tornado which destroys homes, a flood ravages a town, a family member dies, or an unforeseen sickness causes unusual medical expenses. Employees who face crises like these can receive quick assistance from their employer's Employee Assistance Fund (EAF), which typically has the majority of its money donated by the employees themselves. Then there is the other end of the spectrum. You ever hear that the company Overstock has about $10 million in gold, mostly the small button-sized coins, that they keep outside of the banking system. Their CEO says they expect that when there is a financial crisis there will be a banking holiday. They don't know if it will be 2 days, or 2 weeks, or 2 months. But they have $10 million in gold and silver in denominations small enough that OverStock can use for payroll. They want to be able to keep their employees paid, safe and their site up and running during a financial crisis. They also happen to have three months of food supply for every employee that they can live on." Hogan declared ordering one more drink before Boss closed out his tab.

'We need to talk more about that later, I already increased our petty cash at various locations after your suggestions but it is in no way enough to cover any payroll." Boss said eying his bill and adding the tip.

"Hey back to your Country Club idea, do you know a couple of those things are already being built in Texas and Ohio? They cost about 300 million dollars each; the houses are 90 % underground and going for about 6 figures each. The sites are like 700 acres with a 12 ft wall around them complete with guard towers." Hogan said trying to decide if he wanted to walk on home or hang out with the lounge lizards awhile longer.

"I hadn't seen that, email me some articles please, I don't have anything that grandiose in mind but I can see the potential for upgrading their preparedness and expanding into the surrounding community. Do I see you having more interest in my project now?" Boss said pouncing on the subject.

"I never said I wasn't disinterested in it, I just don't want to have to live in the big city to help get it done. If I could work from home and visit, then we got potential. Hey are you going to play the Walt Disney options game?" Hogan said referring to the genius way Disneyland got built.

"You just remember now that we got ourselves a non-circumvent agreement with each other and your work you do for me. That's a touchy subject and not one I care to discuss with you but I might see to it you get a little action on something like that if you are being supportive enough." Boss said a bit miffed that Hogan was eying his secret plans so closely without him even bringing up the subject.

"Mums the word Boss, don't worry about me I was just curious. I really think you are on to something here. I am a player to do what you want except for that move we got to discuss later. Have a good weekend." Hogan said reaching over in order to shake the man's hand.

"What are you doing this weekend, Hogan? Want to come see my compound and make some more suggestions over a big dinner and some relaxation?"" Boss offered.

"No, I appreciate that wonderful offer a whole lot but I have myself a little fishing trip and picnic planned that's kind of important. Hopefully it's going to be one humdinger of a fish catching expedition that I can get video for my YouTube channel but I don't know if I am using the right theory yet. Oh by the way did you download the solar storm notification apps to your phone I gave you? I am curious if Solar storms affect how the fish bite and tomorrow looks like a good day to find out and do some line wetting research. I say they do but I don't know if it will be a positive or negative thing, we already know they affect people's health and emotions as well as cause earthquakes, so it ought to be an interesting experiment." Hogan said as he walked Boss to the door and decided he would head on home himself.

"I forgot to ask you about those things! Those notifications have been driving me nuts. I got them turned off at the moment I was getting too far too many notifications, seemed like one an hour." Boss said fishing around in his pockets for his car keys.

"Oh, sorry about that, I should have told you where to set the threshold on notifications. The directions are on the web page on a little scale that tells you what they affect at what level, just crank them up right under big geomagnetic storm indices that affect power grids and ignore the small disruptions. Guess you already know the latest disturbance is supposed to start hitting earth tomorrow." Hogan said as his thoughts shifted to going fishing the next day.

"Oh I know all about that, I must have got 40 notifications telling me just that before I turned the blamed thing off. Are you worried about this particular geomagnetic storm much? Seems like only medium interference coming at our latitude." Boss asked leaning against his car.

"No, Not really, but I am watching that big sun spot starting to turn towards us maybe stirring up the solar winds. These storms are notoriously difficult to predict. At the moment as near as I can tell from what they are saying officially is that Humanity would only have a 12-hour warning window about the arrival of a "coronal mass ejection". I am talking about a powerful one that could damage the National Grid, pipelines and railway switching signals. For this one we got coming towards us tomorrow they already turned some of the observatory satellites away from the sun and put the shields up so they reduce the chances of damage for them in a few hours. They get messed up so does some of our early warning system." Hogan said waving to a friend of his that was about to head into the double doors of the bar.

"I am not so much worried about the radio telescope satellites and losing GPS on the navigation ones for awhile but I can see how lack of weather satellites and navigational aids can cause other problems." Boss said starting to open his car door but closing it as he saw Hogan's female friend approaching.

"Satellite communications are also essential to many daily activities you are not considering that would be at risk from solar storms. Think about it, every time you purchase a gallon of gas with your credit card, that's a satellite transaction." Hogan said before reminding him that this mega disaster plan he was trying to write also included cyber hacking of such.

"Who's your friend? You been holding out on me and find you someone in this big city?" Boss asked as a pretty smiling young woman approached.

"Just a friend, we live in the same complex. Annie, I want you to meet Mr. Frank Salsec my boss that hired me for that business continuity plan I have been telling you about.

The two shook hands and exchanged pleasantries and Annie explained she was meeting some coworkers inside and before excusing herself asked Hogan if he was coming back in.

"I will be back in shortly; glad I bumped into you because I was making an early night out of it and heading home since we were going fishing in the morning." Hogan said before Boss started asking questions.

"Does he have you buying into his solar storm fishing theory too?" Boss said snidely kidding with Hogan.

"Doesn't have to. Actually, I am the one who asked him how solar storms affect fish since it confuses the hell out of bird's migration flights." Annie said beaming.

"Uh yea, I got to give her credit for that one, hadn't considered it until she brought it up. Guess who might be coming to dinner at the Country Club, boss? You see Annie is one of those preppers I was telling you about I might recruit to assist me." Hogan said before Boss started gushing about he didn't know preppers wore pretty dresses instead of decking out in camo, etc.

"What's this about a Country Club dinner?" Annie asked perplexed but evidently happy about the notion.

"I will tell you about it later, I suspect that gaggle of girls approaching is part of your entourage?" Hogan asked as a carful began bailing out and happily chattering at each other.

"No they don't belong to me; actually, we got more guys than girls coming here tonight from that marketing meeting I gave today. Now, back to the Country Club thing, what is it and why am I going?" Annie said with a disarming smile.

"Mr. Salsec here thinks he can drum me up some business if I can convince them the sky is falling at a little dinner party he wants to put on." Hogan began before Annie interrupted.

"Are you going to give a talk on the Kessler Syndrome? I wouldn't miss that for the world! What's the dress code? Hope it's not too formal I don't have the clothes for that!" Annie said suddenly looking dejected.

"Just regular nice business clothes are fine but no frumpy grey or black wool skirts, colorful evening wear if you know what I mean." Boss began before Annie started asking specific clothing questions he dodged by giving her his business card and telling her to chatter at his personal secretary for details.

"What the hell is the Kessler Syndrome, Hogan? The sky can't actually fall from a solar storm can it?" Boss asked as one eyebrow rose, studying him intently.

Before Hogan could get a word out of his mouth, Annie informed him that it didn't even need a solar storm to cause satellites to fall from the sky and was happening naturally now as they spoke but Hogan was researching the effects of State or country sponsored hackers being able to do it with a cyber attack.

"Briefly, The Kessler Syndrome is a theory proposed by NASA scientist Donald J. Kessler in 1978, used to describe a self-sustaining cascading collision of space debris which in turn causes more collisions and wipes out all the satellites like one big pinball bumper game. Everything in low earth orbit is starting to do it and they are doing projections on a 5 yr increase in occurrences. Oh I am sorry Hogan, you got me babbling about that new planning theory you told me about I wasn't supposed to mention yet. I am just fascinated about it because you don't see it in the news much and what with all the hacking going on it wouldn't take much to make satellites start spinning into each other and starting a cataclysmic space war." Annie said looking at him sheepishly.

"Take her with you! If you need another dress just tell the secretary and the two of you can go shopping on me. Don't be crazy Annie, and refuse a free dress now, it's an investment for me to have you dress for success for this meeting. Hey, did Hogan tell you he was going to get a haircut tomorrow?" Boss said congratulating her and teasing Hogan before saying he must really be getting on home to his wife but Hogan better be ready come Tuesday to give him a small briefing paper before going to the party he was planning.

"He has a niece he sponsors in the dress store business." Hogan offered.

"What did I just do?" Annie asked as they waved goodbye to Mr. Salsec as he pulled out.

"Got you a pretty new dress it sounds like and increased the hell out of my work load on a subject I know little about." Hogan fumed.

"I am sorry, I didn't mean to over talk you but that is one hell of an interesting subject you are working on. If you don't want me to go with you, I will understand." Annie said looking crestfallen.

"Oh hell no, you are doing me a huge favor by going. Actually I was kind of worried you wouldn't want to go and hang out with all them stuffed shirt non preppers. Just try to stay off the gun talk and don't bring up the militia. We got to spoon feed these turkeys and put the polish on the preparedness message. You know as well as I do that the bad press on Doomsday Preppers and bunker dwelling survivalists will give us an uphill battle before we even get started. As far as these folks are concerned I am an Emergency Hurricane Planner turned business continuity expert and keep it in that context as hard as it is. You might still not want to come because I don't want to be hearing conversations from you about bug out bags and beans and bullets to them hoity toity folks. Just pretend you're the weather girl or something saying get ready for a cold front and wrap your water pipes and bring in the pets, if you know what I mean." Hogan warned.

"There is nothing wrong with being a member of the militia; it's in the Constitution but I get your drift, Hogan. I won't embarrass you, I will be good, I promise!" Annie said looking puppy eyed at him.

Hogan laughed knowing he was probably shooting himself in the foot by holding her to that promise but the vivacious prepper woman could more than likely hold her own and then some with that high society crowd better than he could. That is if she tried minding her enthusiasm and Ps and Qs on what some considered politically correct prepping. He did have his doubts and pauses about her though and would try to be listening out and rein her in if the subject of community defense or something other than hunting rifles came up.

"Let's go have a drink and meet your people from work." Hogan suggested ready to go have some more fun.

"Ok I agree but only if you don't start chattering about solar storms!" Annie said giving him a playful poke to the ribs to remind him that he wasn't no angel when it came to keeping his own big mouth shut particularly when he already looked a bit tipsy to her.

2

The Day The Sun Brought Darkness To The World

Beep! BEEP! Hogan's computer started droning the second he turned the audio volume on when he woke up blurry eyed and hung over at 7 am. This just after a song called "In A Gadda Da Vida "by Iron Butterfly had already loudly blasted him out of bed on his clock radio alarm this morning.

"What a terribly shockingly LOUD way to wake up! ARRGH! Coffee first and then I will see to the daily news." Hogan thought to himself as he struggled to drag his oversized throbbing head to the stove and turn the kettle on.

He came back to his dining room table and managed to settle down in his chair while trying to view a dizzying array of apps flashing and a full email box as well as a slew of people trying to direct message him on Face Book. He had a hard time trying to focus on just where to start first as evidently something major must have just happened between the time he had drug himself and Annie back from the bar at 3 am this morning and now. *We can do this without the sounds!" Hogan thought and muted them entirely.*

Annie didn't drink much and Hogan often joked that he drank enough for both of them although he rarely showed any hangover effects for doing so, today was different. After only four hours sleep and a very loud wakeup speaker blast had jarred him out of his slumbers, his eyes didn't want to seem to focus and his head had him hurting' for certain today. He had actually tried to call off this fishing trip until a better day or got Annie to consider for them to go much later in the day than planned but she was having none of it. She insisted they get going no later than 7:30 AM and he begrudgingly had agreed.

The prospect of a new dress and country club dinner where Hogan was to be the featured speaker and her to be his honored guest was just too much for her. She could have probably talked about the invite until dawn if Hogan had let her.

Hogan had also promised to show her his newest secret he was keeping regarding the river. He had been as tight lipped as a clam as to what exactly that was but regretted mentioning it at all now as the light of day hit him. The alcohol he had consumed last night had loosened his lips just enough to bring up the subject of showing her something special on the river and now he was going to be paying the early morning price for that indiscretion.

"What in the world did all these flashing tray icons mean on this computer?" Hogan thought as he fuzzily hit the most recognizable one as a space weather alert. Best to know how it would affect his solar storm fishing theory today, he reckoned.

"Holy Crap! This ain't good!" Hogan said out loud as he leaned forward hurriedly to read a number and began to read the first message that came up. Coronal Mass Ejection alert!

"Uncool! Unfreaking cool! This is bad, oh this is very bad!" Hogan mumbled to himself and then hurried to un-mute the sound on his audible warnings on his business cell phone which was sitting on the kitchen counter.

According to a quick perusal of immediate action warnings, it appeared NASA had just recently issued a 24 hour warning of a CME hitting earth and that all electrical producing companies were supposed begin to power down their reactors and turbines by 10:00. He no sooner just had started to register that fact and reach for his next button app when a heavy pounding started on his door that sounded like the cops wanted to come in while his phone also immediately started ringing.

"Hang on a second!" Hogan yelled as he grabbed his phone and tried to make sense in his mind what he had done with his pants last night before going to bed and located his personal cell phone and answered it.

"I'm coming!" Hogan yelled as he fished his phone out of his jeans change pocket and said hello while trying to fit one leg into them at the same time.

"Hey it's Frank Salsec! Do you know what's going on?" The excited voice of his Boss said through the receiver.

"Just got up buddy, but yes I do! Shit is about to hit the fan right? Hang on a second I got to answer the door." Hogan said as his befuddled brain tried to get his other pants leg on while evidently Annie was trying to break down his door and in his haste to get dressed and answer it he wound up falling on the bed.

"Damn boots!" Hogan called out as he tripped over those too and stepped on a pebble that evidently the aggressive treads of those things had picked up and left in his path for his bare feet to find.

"Are you there?" Bosses voice called in his ear from the phone he had jammed to his head.

"I am working on it, hold tight, Boss." Hogan called back to the receiver and the voice outside his door.

"Hogan, its happening! Let me in, watch out!" THUMP! THUMP! The loud knocking resumed as Annie called to him as she rushed by his disheveled looking self and went to turn on his TV where the emergency broadcast system had begun to blare its warnings as soon as it had warmed up a second.

"Turn that crap off or at least turn it down a bunch Annie, I got a call here I am on!" Hogan yelled out as she pranced between the TV and his computer to see what news he had up on screen.

"Hogan, we got less than 12 hours to prepare for lights out!" A distraught Boss hollered into the phone with a couple expletives added to tell him he needed to get his hungover butt in gear.

"Boss, I got to call you back. Sorry but I don't know up from down or what's going on until I get to my computer for a few minutes." Hogan started to say before the TV and all the lights went out.

"Wouldn't you know it? Power just went out; stay on the phone I don't know when the cell towers will quit. Tell you what, go to the store before the panic sets in and get groceries." Hogan began to say before Annie said give me your wallet, evidently offering to help him with that advice.

"Both of you quit talking for a second!" Hogan bellowed trying to wrap his head around what was happening.

"Zip your zipper." Annie advised ignoring his request and went to look in his kitchen cabinets evidently thinking more clearly than he was.

"I take that back Boss, you need to stay indoors, don't get out on the roads at all because you already got enough food stored to see you through." Hogan managed to get out before the line went dead as millions of people nationwide started calling their friends and relatives overloading the phone system.

"Crap, I will try calling him back later, what did you hear on that emergency broadcast?" Hogan asked as Annie flitted around looking out windows and looking more nervous than a rattle snakes tail as Hogan tried to take in what all was happening.

"What do we do, Hogan?" Annie asked beseechingly.

"Hell I don't know! Quit yelling at me for one thing. So I am not dreaming and this is the real deal emergency I been warning folks was going to happen someday, right?" Hogan asked knowing it was but wanting confirmation.

"I just got up this morning a short while ago also but the TV emergency bulletin had an official space weather emergency warning on it that said that the electricity would be turned off in a few hours and tune to our local emergency broadcast stations for future notices. I guess they meant radios because the cable channels said they would be going off line after updating shortly." Annie said looking like a baseball player trying to think about stealing second and doing the half move in that direction thing between Hogan's desk and the front door. Where she wanted to go Hogan didn't know exactly but figured it was to the grocery store but it soon became apparent she wanted to get back to her apartment and load more of her preps into her car.

"I got my bug out bag ready and emptied my pantry into pillow cases. What should I do next, Hogan?" Annie asked as she checked the pistol he hadn't noticed she was wearing at her side under the long shirt tail of a Khaki shirt she had on.

"Where in the world do you plan on bugging out to? You know these roads are going to be all clogged up in seconds if they aren't already jammed up leading into the city now. How much cash have you got on you? We can go to the corner convenience store and load up if it doesn't look too bad. If it's packed, we bypass it and try to hit the Food Lion for some canned goods are the only two things I can think of." Hogan said studying the full size pistol she was barely concealing.

"We have only got just twelve hours to get away they say, why don't we leave now to and head to your place in Alabama?" Annie asked.

"Dang give me a minute. I don't think that's possible to do safely right at the moment." Hogan said as he went to his backpack and pulled out a crank and battery/solar powered radio.

Once he got the batteries loaded and tuned in to a local station, they both listened intently to the emergency broadcast streaming out reports for a few minutes. A national Emergency had been declared with warnings to prepare for extended power and water outages. People were advised to stay home and not go out unless absolutely necessary and listen to the Presidents Emergency address to the Nation in an hour it said. Traffic reports when Hogan found one were scanty but were pretty much as he bad he guessed with temporary road closures and wrecks.

"Fat lot of good that will do!" Annie began to say regarding the instructions on stay indoors before the power suddenly came back on and the TV began to stream its annoying alert noises and recorded warnings again.

"I guess some of the power stations hit the off switch a bit too early! Ok what we need to do is get ready to bug ourselves in here and not be thinking about bugging out just yet. Everyone at the moment is going to be losing their minds on the road and I bet it gets even worse the later it gets. Let's go try to get ourselves some food if we can and see what the traffic is doing. If it looks like we can get a clear path out of here, we will just go ahead and leave now before the interstate exits shut down. You are welcome as you know to go hide out at my prepper shack for as long as it takes but I bet the roads out of here are snarled already from that brief power outage. People are fools even when the streetlights are working properly. I bet a lot of places and intersections are already screwing up by the numbers if the traffic lights have been off at all." Hogan declared.

"I started hearing ambulances and such at about six thirty. I am not sure just how long they have been broadcasting the initial warning." Annie said as the power began blipping on and off before finally staying off.

"How are you fixed on water?" Hogan asked as he went to fill up his bathtub.

"I have already done that and have filled most every pot and pan in the house with water. Want me to start filling up yours? Feels weird to do that with the river so close by but I remembered what you said about the pollution that might be coming downstream if the power stayed off awhile." Annie said before Hogan's phone began to ring and Annie's too.

"Hogan, try to get to me, scratch, scratch electronic noise, if you can make it, garble, garble #%@" and then his phone went dead again as well as Annie's.

"That was my family trying to see if I was alright." Annie said beginning to cry but still dutifully filling up Hogan's pots and pans with precious tap water.

"It will be ok, Darling, we will get through this." Was all Hogan could come up with to say as he stopped her from her task momentarily and held her for a few seconds, overwhelmed at both of their current state of affairs.

The radio droned on in the background with local traffic reports interrupted by emergency broadcast messages that said nothing other than we were in for deep doo doo and for citizens to get water and supplies if they could.

"Great, no water pressure." Hogan said as his faucets flow turned to a trickle.

"Dang it! I had the perfect way out of this mess a moment ago I thought because my boss said for me to come to his house to ride it out. We would have been sitting pretty there, but the radio just said traffic was hopelessly snarled from Buford highway and beyond with Forest Park cutoff closed from a semi accident and fires at the airport. Come on, you can leave that for later lets go to the convenience store." Hogan said grabbing his keys and as they exited his apartment he could see other people must have woken up and heard the same broadcast they had.

"Maybe not! Look at all those people rushing to get out! Let's just stay here at home for awhile until the parking lot clears and avoid the accidents and work on what we got on hand. How are you fixed for food?" Hogan asked Annie.

"The usual, it's the end of the week and I was going to go shopping Sunday after we went fishing today to do the re-supply. I haven't got anything much at all stored for preps here except 72 hours in my bug out bag and maybe a weeks' worth of odd meals from buying an extra item or two every week when I go to the grocery store to build up something around here food prep wise. I am kind of like you; I had to leave all my long term storage food preps at home to move over here for a short while." Annie said wringing her hands.

"Well some folks call me crazy but I got 45 lbs. each of beans and rice in five gallon buckets I threw in the back of my van coming up here as back up preps. I will be proud to share those with you and I even got two cases of spam, one of which just got delivered by Amazon yesterday. Other than that, my pantry is kind of lacking but I got a solid week or two worth of basic canned goods like soups and ravioli and such." Hogan said contemplating their next move.

"I thought you might have something crazy like that put back and I am so glad that you do and offered to share! However, as grateful as I am that doesn't tell me what our next step is, what are you thinking, Hogan? That food won't last as long as this problem is going to be going on. I think we need to be leaving out now, don't we?" Annie declared and looked to her friend for some miraculous advice she knew wasn't forthcoming but had to ask anyway.

"Gimme a bit. Hey coffee water is still hot, want some?" Hogan asked.

"Oh that would be wonderful. I was in such a hurry to get my stuff together and packed and get over here that I missed my cup this morning." Annie replied appearing much more calmed down as their mutual plight registered and a plan of action started to be made and discussed.

"First things first, let's deal with our most imminent dangers." Hogan said as he poured her a cup of coffee.

"We are avoiding danger by not getting out at the moment. No sense foolishly charging out in this mess if we don't have to right this minute. Hey you want a shot of whiskey in your coffee? I shouldn't be even thinking of doing one but I need a bit of the hair of the dog to clear my head after last night. Damn your friends can drink!" Hogan said making a small joke that didn't go over very well.

"No I don't want one but you go ahead. Liquor store?" Annie asked thinking of barter material and less likely places to visit that would be not flooded with customers at this hour maybe.

"Good idea but they don't open until 10 o'clock and that's if they are coming in to work at all today but add that to your list." Hogan said thinking that was a very good idea seeing he only had a half of bottle himself in the apartment to make it through the whole apocalypse. Hey they carried ice and snacks also in that store so why not?

"How much ammo you got on hand?" Annie questioned.

"Enough, we ain't going to try to go to the gun store or Wal-Mart, if that's what you're thinking. Besides I only have 24 dollars or so in cash on me and who knows what the credit cards are doing today." Hogan said dismissing the idea.

"How much cash do you have anyway?" Hogan inquired.

"I have over $300 I got put back and some in my purse left from last night I will count now." Annie said going to look.

"Looks like I got $363, what can we go buy?" Annie asked trying to think.

"Give me a minute to let this drink unfrazzle my nerves some; I can't believe I didn't replace my reserve cash I spent the other day instead of going to the bank. Annie what business is close and open in the next hour or so that we haven't mentioned yet?" Hogan said studying the problem more closely.

"How about going to the pet store?" Annie exclaimed.

"Yea let's think about sitting on their doorstep pretty soon. I can eat sunflower seeds just as well as a bird can and I ain't objecting to us buying some cans of Alpo dog food to eat if we have to. There isn't anything around here to consider that's close other than every kind of food restaurant imaginable. I wonder if we ought to maybe try to buy some of their uncooked inventory if the price is right. That is if we can find someone willing to sell us something. No bad idea, no one will probably even show up for work anyway to open up." Hogan said looking out the window at the unusual amount of traffic moving around in the complex.

Annie joined him at the window and looked out also.

"I got to say it, You know if this event wasn't so tragic and bizarre it would be kind of fun and interesting as an emergency drill to speculate on what everyone is doing or thinking about doing at the moment. What do people do when they find out their world collapses in 12 hours?" Annie murmured.

"So far they aren't freaking out around here too bad. A lot of people have some kind of stupid media induced idea we all turn into manic gibbering idiots at the first sign of danger manifesting itself when I have found exactly the opposite is true." Hogan said noticing people were pretty much driving normally and allowing each other to pass and go on when in doubt.

"Come on Hogan, we can figure things out in the car. I will be careful driving but we are getting in on this great big going out of business sale somehow while we can maybe still find something." Annie said taking her belt off to change the position of her hip holster to a small of the back carry rig.

"NEAT! A multi position holster, that's a pretty slick setup, Annie. I saw one of those things advertised in Sportsman's Guide once but I have never seen one in person. By the way, I was going to say something to you about it before we took off. I don't think just because the emergency broadcast system said hell starts in 12 hours means you can open carry in this town just yet." Hogan said while pondering if besides just his concealed carry Keltec 9mm he should grab his full size pistol and waistband carry it because all he only had was a shoulder holster for it.

It was hot as could be moving towards the 90's now it felt like and he really didn't want to try wearing an extra shirt over that shoulder holster to try to conceal it. He noted his pistol carrying quandary to Annie who was all for him just wearing a t-shirt and putting on an open denim short sleeved work shirt over it because it didn't seem to print the material too badly. She cautioned him however to just be careful if he leaned over so he wouldn't be flashing the piece too much.

" I ain't too worried about needing more than my little pocket rocket pistol but today I bet is going to be idiot day for everyone to be packing a pistol so I better have with me a bit more firepower on me, I guess. I am telling you right now though Annie, if that grocery store looks and acts like a Black Friday sale door buster special of people running over and trampling each other, we ain't going to go near it. Those kinds of unruly crowds would mean we already got the poorer outlying neighborhoods already checking out the resources in this richer side of town and they tend to have the want to be gangster types with them that like to shoot up stuff for no reason and act like fools no matter what." Hogan said as they walked down to her car.

Hogan had advised Annie before he believes the most violent people-at least in the early stages of SHTF are going to be some of the more clueless young people and those on Welfare or other entitlement programs. Mostly he believed this to be true because generally speaking these people have NO concept of putting back supplies or are able to try to save some funds. They will be the first to become hungry, the first to make screaming demands on others, and the first to turn violent when they realize the gravy train of food stamps or other assistance isn't running anymore.

"You got a long gun hid somewhere in there?" Hogan asked eying the evidently packed to the gills little rental car her company had provided for her stay.

"No damn it, all of mine are back at home in Missouri. It was hard enough for me just bringing my pistol here because they flew me in. I could have maybe figured something out to get a long gun here but it was just too much trouble. You know what they say about hindsight. Besides I had an assigned company representative come pick me up at the airport and I didn't want to start any gossip the first day here with a checked rifle or shotgun I needed to retrieve from the baggage claim. I did think about though, I considered I might get away with saying I was a skeet shooter and bringing my shotgun but I decided against it. Anything that might be related to a rifle case freaks folks in my corporate world out." Annie said with a sigh.

"Throw your bug out bag inside my house at least and leave us some room in your backseat in case we manage to score some groceries." Hogan said regarding the jumble of gear he saw in the car and mentally knowing that her trunk was equally packed.

"Yea Ok, I forgot how pretty much loaded up my car was. I figured me and you would have already been on the highway by now. You sure you don't want to reconsider doing that?" Annie said still wondering if trying to drive out wasn't their best move but being so far from home she was going to stick to Hogan like glue and follow his lead because of his many years experience of being a master of disaster in situations similar to this.

"I am still arguing with myself on that one, but we know the power has been flickering on and off for some time now and in my opinion it only takes only once or twice and five minutes of no streetlights for Atlanta downtown to get into a huge mess of dodge the bumper impassable intersections and folks wrecking." Hogan said.

"I see your point; you think we will be alright going out on the roads now?" Annie questioned.

"I ain't all that keen to try it, but I am willing to try if you are since we are in the suburbs and there is no ice on the roads to mess the speeders up. You remember when it snowed back in January or were you here then?" Ok you missed the fun, the whole damn city was shut down for days from a little snow and folks lost their minds sliding around or just stayed home waiting it out. Nobody knew how to drive in it; since I had driven in snow and ice before I used to make grocery runs for about a week for others because a lot of people in this complex couldn't get out or back up that steep hill entering here." Hogan declared as Annie opened her backdoor.

"Want to take your van instead?" Annie asked.

"No, it's loaded to the hilt too. We were supposed to go fishing today remember? I got the ice chest, fish rods, my inflatable boat, motor; you name it in there." Hogan said thinking in some kind of bizarre way it was pretty cool he was mostly already loaded up for a bug out if he thought about all that gear that way. What sucked was he was all ready to leave in an instant and he couldn't get anywhere.

"I forgot you been riding that raft of yours around and a bunch of other camping stuff since you been here." Annie began before Hogan complained it wasn't a "raft" it was an inflatable boat with a keel and a transom and everything and that the Navy Seals didn't attack beaches on rafts they did it on Zodiac type boats. Besides it was called a Sport Runabout if she wanted to get technical.

"Don't be so touchy, I know what it is and I like the hell out of it. I wish I had one. I just always call it your lifeboat or life raft and occasionally interchange the word raft. I know how technologically advanced and tough that boat is. I buy from the same company Sea Eagle, don't you know!" Annie said a bit miffed that Hogan was being such a stickler about what she called his boat but he was right. Maybe he was just being prickly about it because waking up to this crap with the mung head would make anyone testy. Secretly she was glad though that she was driving and not him because Hogan had refilled his drink again and brought it with him. He wasn't even close to being drunk but he had said he needed to put it down soon as a drink that early in the morning coming off the party of last night had him feeling it but it was the apocalypse so what the hell? He could have one if she was driving and he wanted it.

The convenience store looked like an ant pile that had been kicked, evidently the power must have come back on because folks were trying to fill up their gas tanks as well as buy sundries.

"Wouldn't that be the pits?" Hogan remarked as he turned to look back "Just imagine Annie to be trying to fill your tank with the power going on and off? I mean you get a couple dollars worth and the power shuts off, a long line of cars is waiting in back of you wanting gas and the pump suddenly isn't doing anything. Do you leave it and drive off or do you attempt to stand around until it comes back on?" Hogan asked.

"Sounds to me like one of those conflicted card game questions but you got a point there. I wouldn't know what to do." Annie said referring to a prepper pastime in some community get-togethers of playing a game based on a certain circumstance and talking out various options and scenarios to survive it amongst the other participants.

Hogan had a full tank of gas in his van because he had filled up the day before to go fishing. The plan was to put his boat in far downriver where he hadn't explored yet but that wasn't happening today. One nice thing about having an inflatable was no need for boat ramps to launch from because he didn't need to drag it around on a trailer.

Annie had her Sea Eagle 370 Kayak that could take advantage of all different types of just plain old river bank entry points also. As a matter of fact, it was that Kayak of hers that had brought them together and made them the friends that they were now.

Hogan had seen an advertisement in the apartment complexes newsletter that said "Want to Learn to Kayak? Group accepts members' 8-80." and he had went to a Kayak and Canoe livery on the river to check it out. Annie was already a member and after he had rented one of the establishments solid kayaks and took a few lessons he had gotten to talking to her and found out they lived in the same apartment complex. He had asked her if she minded him taking her inflatable kayak for a short paddle with her because he was considering buying one. He felt like If he was going to keep pursuing the Kayak thing for recreation it would come out cheaper for him in the long run to own his own Kayak and he had no place to store a big plastic regular one like he had been renting. He thought something like Annie's Kayak might be a perfect match for kayaking with the clubs in the Atlanta area. Well after that brief trial excursion they had started palling around a little bit just as friends and kind of became close prepper buddies over the months happily chattering about all things prepping and sharing several drinks or a meal here and there.

Annie even had another couple who tried hers out with their dog and enjoyed it so much they bought one.

Hogan's 10.6' Sport Runabout was the best kind of boat for fishing the river though and they cut quite a picture playing with it launching it from the river access at the apartment building. It wasn't the best place in the world to launch from but it was free and convenient and generally speaking no one ever used it. It was more of a worn path on a short piece of beach and trail that dog walkers and playing kids had tramped down over time more than anything else.

The two boaters were about 20 years different in age but it didn't affect their friendship any except when Annie playfully joked at him about lifting something or doing something he was griping about being harder than it looked.

"Come on old man!" she would say and lend him a hand picking up something heavy or get him to push himself a little further on a long paddle if he started talking about taking it easier if she wanted to go fast versus slow in her tandem kayak.

Annie kept her Kayak in her trunk and it weighed an amazingly light 32 lbs. That particular Kayak packs down small enough to fit in the smallest car trunk. Don't let the light weight fool you, it's a rugged kayak able to hold 3 people or 650 lbs and yet easy enough to be carried and paddled by one. It could even be sailed downwind because she had bought that neat accessory to play with and enjoy.

Hogan's boat on the other hand was larger and as safe and seaworthy as an inflatable boat can be made. He had spared no expense getting what he wanted in comfort and mobility in one package. He wanted something very durable to stand the test of time and be able to haul cargo and people easily.

He had certainly found those characteristics in this one because the overall base hull weight of

90 lbs. while still able to carry 5 adults or an amazing 1200 lbs. with ease. He had purchased an excellent fishing boat as well as a tough reliable prepper bug out boat with some functional class, in his opinion.

His weighed 78 lbs. (hull), 90 lbs. (w/ inflatable floor installed) he could move it around by himself but it sure was easier with another set of hands to help. Two people could easily carry it inflated but he solo boated a lot and eventually got himself some wheels to drag it around if he wanted to.

Hogan and she had gotten on the subject of using their watercraft as excursion camping or bug out boats, a subject he was already well versed in.

That was the reason he had made sure he got to live on this river when he moved up here. That was why he had chosen his particular Sea Eagle boat for recreation as well as emergency transportation use.

It was in his studied opinion that his best chance of survival was to use the Chattahoochee River as his escape route out of the city should he find the road ways blocked. The Chattahoochee runs all the way to Florida but is not navigable the entire distance without pulling out here and there and portaging around things. The current plan of his was sort of dead ended by that fact but he wasn't sure how far down he could actually travel without the need to avoid something. He knew the official kayak river trail ran 45 miles out of Atlanta and of course there were off shoots like the Flint River and various creeks but he didn't know what was waiting for him at the end of the road navigable water passage wise.

He hadn't found the time to explore that far downriver yet nor buy any maps that detailed that region. All he knew that south was the direction of his escape and the way he wanted to go to get out of the city as fast as he could avoiding the highways. He kicked himself for that bit of un-preparedness right now but it couldn't be helped. He had a general map showing all the rivers' contours but it was a highway map and didn't indicate hardly anything about true river conditions.

"Turn right up here, I have a back way we can use to get to the grocery store. Don't know why I didn't think of going this way before. You got to cut through the back of the shopping center to get there but that might work out to our advantage. I wonder if anyone will be doing any deliveries today. Might sound stupid but what is a trucker going to do if he has a load scheduled to be dropped off today. Does he drop it and haul ass home, turn around and take the trailer with him knowing it contains food or what?" Hogan asked and they pondered the question.

"No telling, if I was the trucker I would be wondering if anybody was going to show up to work today to unload the truck or open the store at all." Annie offered.

"Guess we get to see soon enough, hang a left on that service road and just wrap on around towards the back of the building." Hogan said giving directions while looking around for any signs of big rigs. Two more cars decided to use the same road they were on but they turned off to go to the front of the stores as Hogan and Annie carried on with their mission to explore the back lots first. There weren't any parked trucks back there but there were a couple cars parked in back of the dollar store and they apparently were loading up their vehicles with stuff out of the back door.

"Careful, this situation can get real touchy quickly. Stop here a minute." Hogan said about 50 yards off from the activity.

"Looks like the employees maybe are having themselves their very own pre-looting day sale." Annie declared studying the people.

"Got your pistol handy?" Hogan asked already knowing she had put it under her seat when she got in but not knowing how fast she could get to it.

"Yea I got it, what's the plan?" Annie said fishing under her seat and not liking any part of what was going on in back of that store.

"We are going to wave to them and act all friendly like and I am going to hold up some cash and see if they will parlay. Evidently they got the front door locked and the lights turned off to repel any would be customers, I am guessing. What I don't like thinking about is what type of answer that manager looking type standing over there eying us with what is probably a chrome plated .357 revolver on his hip might say. Probably, he will just run us off and wave and tell us to go away so be ready for that and just leave if he says so." Hogan said assessing the situation.

"Ok, here goes nothing." Annie said driving slowly forward towards the group.

"Hey, isn't that one of the Yak boys over there? I think his name is Danny." Hogan said looking at a young man carrying boxes out.

"Yea that's Danny! Whew this doesn't sound so crazy to be coming over here now." Annie said relieved they had seen somebody they knew from their Kayaking group. This particular individual floated from this group to that one at another landing but Hogan had labeled him and his millennial daredevil buddies the Yak boys because they were your typical young Georgia yuppie river rats that could have easily turned out as California dude surfer types had they been raised on the opposite coast and played with surfboards instead of kayaks.

Hogan waved cash; Annie called out to Danny and Mr. .357 magnum manager type seemed to relax a little.

Danny and the manager walked over to the car and told them the store was closed due to power outages and to hearing this obvious news Annie whined they didn't need much and Hogan cajoled the manager that they would pay whatever it took to get supplies.

Annie waving her $200 must have looked good to the manager because he finally conceded to let them have some stuff but it was pricy. They could have two hand baskets of canned goods and Danny would get sent to get them for them. They were not going to be allowed to come in the closed store they were informed. Danny assured them that he would pick out some good stuff and he did. He grabbed pretty much what any seasoned camping Kayaker would want and threw in extra wherever he could.

While Danny was inside the store getting their groceries, Hogan talked the manager into giving him a case of beer for $25 bucks because that's all the money he had and evidently the manager took a liking to him or just felt magnanimous because he gave him two cases and wished him good luck before they left.

"Well that turned out to be painless. Way to go, Hogan, for thinking of coming to the backdoor before going to the front door! You should of tried to get more food instead of that beer though." Annie said as they began to exit the parking lot not even bothering to see what kind of melee was going on over at the grocery store in the front of the place.

"Hey beer has calories in it! Hold up a minute, slow down and honk your horn at those folks, Annie. That's Mr. Wong from the Chinese takeout food place that is heading this way!" Hogan said pointing at a small blue Toyota pickup truck with a camper shell on it.

"No time to talk today, Hogan! I got to go! Must get to the restaurant!" An apparently overly rushed and excited Chinese man said with a thick accent.

"Won't keep you but a minute Mr. Wong, can I trouble you to sell me a sack of flour, please? I got a Silver dollar to trade!" Hogan said with a big smile reminding the man he was a regular patron and had once given a silver dollar as a tip to his cook for an exceptional meal and had given another to his wife as a present when she had become a full fledged U.S. citizen.

Mr. Wong turned to his wife and chattered something in Mandarin and he turned to Hogan and said yes to follow them as his wife gave Hogan a thumbs up.

"Well we are just batting a thousand today, our lucky day it seems in spite of that solar flare!" Annie said as she waved at the waitress and cook following Mr. Wong she also recognized in the other car and got turned around.

Before they got out of the car, Hogan reached around to the back seat and pulled out a six pack of still somewhat cold beer and offered one to Mr. Wong when he got out.

The proprietor took it from him just to be courteous it seemed and held it unopened as did the cook who eventually soon enough opened his and took a swig while the two ladies demurely said no thanks.

"You have Dollah for me?" Mrs. Wong said in her gruff Asian accent

"Got it right here!" Hogan said handing the shiny coin over to the admiring women's hands as they followed them in the back door of the restaurant.

Hogan had never heard the cook speak English before and they had been mugging at each other and using sign language of sorts for months so they had their own form of understanding one another. There was a tiny five stool mini bar around the corner from the takeout corner and Hogan would hang out at it once in awhile as the cook doubled as bartender occasionally.

You and Lady want a drink he motioned while looking to his boss for an ok which he got but in many more words than seemed necessary.

"Uh, you want a drink?" Hogan asked Annie thinking what the hell, be the last one he ever got in this place and hanging around here as the owners were evidently going to carry some food off or something might prove profitable or beneficial.

"Yes sure as long it is ok with Mrs. Wong and her husband?" Annie said looking over at the pair to which Mrs. Wong hearing her name being mentioned first immediately stepped forward motioning with her hand for them to have a seat as she reached for the whiskey to make Hogan his usual Jack and Coke while asking Annie what she wanted and was pleased to hear the "same."

A torrent of Chinese started up as the restaurant operators chattered at each other incessantly and left Hogan and Annie sitting there all by their lonesome as they tended to the kitchen with the opening of coolers and slamming of cabinets.

"I don't have any cash for these drinks." Hogan whispered to Annie.

"I know that, I didn't know you had any silver on you." Annie whispered back.

"I got four silver dollars left and a roll of dimes left." Hogan confided.

"I got three ounces of silver in my bug out bag back at the apartment but that's it." Annie said in a hushed tone back.

"Then we are wealthy." Hogan said with a grin.

"Think we can get anything else here?" Annie asked still whispering.

"I have no idea, flour was all I could think of when I saw them, they usually use fresh ingredients to cook with I think." Hogan replied.

"I don't think you need any more to drink, Hogan, if you're asking a Chinese restaurant if you can buy flour from them instead of rice." Annie said in a mock scolding voice before tittering at the expression Hogan got on his face for not thinking of it until now.

"Ah hell I had boiled noodles on the brain, I eat them every time I come in so I was thinking of them and how the hell we might be able to make them and wontons and dumplings and such first. DUH! Can't believe I missed the obvious." Hogan began to say before someone tried the front door awful loudly.

Annie jumped a mile and Mr. Wong suddenly appeared with a 1911 .45 pistol in the kitchen doorway as a group of teenagers appeared at the glass front door motioning they wanted to come in.

"We Closed! We Closed!" Mr. Wong said waving them away.

"I don't like leaving my gun out in the car." Annie whispered.

"I got two, we are going to be gone in a few minutes but I will tell Mr. Wong to be sure his backdoor is locked if it isn't already." Hogan said.

"I hear you, Hogan. Doors locked, those bad boys wanting to get in here, trouble." Mr. Wong said now walking back towards them with a look over his shoulder to see if any more scowling faces appeared to contest his restaurant being closed to the public.

"I have a drink with you, Hogan, and then we all go home. You come back in kitchen where no one sees you though." Mr. Wong said asking them to move away from the bar.

"No problem." Annie and Hogan said heading that way carrying their drinks.

Mr. Wong put his pistol into his waistband under his vest and opened the beer Hogan had given him that he had sat inside the melting ice machine

"Bad times are coming, Hogan, best we don't stay here too long." Mr. Wong said as his wife and the rest of the help went on stacking stuff next to the back door.

"To better times!" Hogan said giving him a glass to can cheers which they shared with Annie.

"You stay around and help guard until cousins come and help load vehicles I give you boo coo Chinese take out!" Mr. Wong said with a big smile then he translated what he said to the rest of the group and everyone had a nervous big laugh.

"I do." the cook said and started filling up a flat cardboard box with little take out containers.

"Damn, he does speak English a little." Hogan murmured as he gave the man thumbs up and was rewarded with a crazy happy gap-tooth grin in return.

"Go get your gun, Annie, looks like we are on kitchen guarding duty." Hogan said starting to rise to accompany her but Cook waved for him to sit back down and produced an ancient Police .38 special revolver and walked back to stick his head out the door and motion Annie to come on.

"We are going to the mountains, Hogan; you wait here for a minute, please." Mr. Wong said slipping out to go to the bar and coming back with a bottle of Peppermint Schnapps and four shot glasses which he dutifully filled and called his wife over while they waited for Annie to return.

"We always go to mountains in times of trouble or running from the Communists." Mr. Wong stated as Annie came back and eyed the shot glasses lined up on the bar wondering what was up.

"Where you and woman go, Hogan?" Mr. Wong asked handing a glass to his wife and Annie and signaling everyone bottoms up.

Hogan couldn't help but make a small face as the fiery peppermint flavored drink hit the back of his throat and the taste conflicted with his whiskey but he forced a smile anyway.

"The river most likely, I am thinking the world will be on fire tomorrow or tonight. Run to the mountains quick my friend because the traffic will stop soon." Hogan said and at a curious look from his wife Mr. Wong translated.

"I tell her emergency man warn of us of traffic jam and fire coming soon. She no understands you talking about fire, wants to know if it be fire come from sky like dragon moon, I think she mean meteorite." Mr. Wong said before jabbering at her again in Chinese.

"She says no mean sun fire like radiation maybe." Mr. Wong said scrutinizing him.

"No radiation to worry about that affects humans; the city is going to burn down because of no Fire Department communications and water pressure." Hogan said and motioned with his hands like he was doing Indian sign language palm down like a house burning to the ground to which the cook got it and started jabbering at his wife.

"Cook wants to know if the fire will be everywhere even in the mountains. I think he is saying will the fire be coming from sky?" Mr. Wong said.

"No fire won't be coming down from the sky; it will be coming from the transformers on the telephone poles." Hogan stated still regretting drinking that Schnapps but it wasn't too bad after all when it settled and maybe he would ask for another.

"I don't think they know what an electrical transformer is." Annie whispered as a confused sing song of language went on to their ears.

"You got a pen?" Hogan asked and Annie fished one out of her purse to which he started drawing a power pole on a bar napkin with a lightning bolt hitting the transformer.

"Ah!" everyone exclaimed looking at the picture.

"Well the lightening is invisible you won't see it." Hogan managed to explain to what he hoped was acknowledging head nods.

Hogan, you want uncooked Cab fishes to take home? Free, they be no good to eat tomorrow with no refrigeration." Mrs. Wong said.

"Sure, thank you!" Hogan exclaimed with a big grin.

"What's a "Cabs Fishes?" Annie asked which made Mr. Wong laugh uproariously until he managed to explain.

"She no can say soft-shell Crabs which Hogan always orders fried in tempura when he comes in. She calls crabs cabs. Take a bunch of them if you want, you got friends? I got some fish and other things that will be no good soon without ice." Mr. Wong offered.

"I uh, umm, No I don't think so, wouldn't know what to do with more than we could eat tonight. Annie?" Hogan said looking inquiringly at his friend.

"Wow, got me on that one, I barely know my neighbors. If they are just going to leave it here I suppose we could try to give some away back at the complex." Annie said questionably.

"Any other time I wouldn't hesitate and would welcome the chance to help someone out but I don't want to start getting all friendly to strangers that hardly speak to me." Hogan said trying to get out of taking anything extra with them.

"My neighbors are nice; Hogan is it ok if I move in with you? You are closer to the river side and I think it's safer if we stay together and watch each other's backs." Annie asked knowing the answer would be yes.

"No problem, I was going to suggest that anyway. Give your neighbors some fish and shrimp if you want and tell them you're leaving if you want but not where you got the food from. Mr. Wong, you wouldn't consider selling some whiskey for a silver dollar would you or maybe let me buy some nice rice?" Hogan asked hoping he wasn't pushing the envelope too far with all the hospitality shown already.

"Two silver dollars?" Mrs. Wong asked smiling and extending her hand.

"Two it is then, this one I will keep for luck." Hogan said reaching in his pocket and pulling out three coins.

"Good deal, Hogan!" Mr. Wong said shaking his hand and the cook moved a 50 lb. sack of rice to the pile Hogan and Annie were accumulating while Mr. Wong retrieved for him a full half gallon of whiskey and a bonus of part of an open jug and set it down in front of Hogan.

"Good Deal, Mr. Wong. I am sure going to miss this place a lot. Especially the prices!" Hogan said offering to do cheers with his glass to Mr. and Mrs. Wong again.

"Let's start helping them load up, I saw a couple people looking in the window again a few minutes ago." Annie said bringing everyone back to the ground and attending to the problems at hand.

Annie and Hogan got her car loaded first, grabbed a box of soy sauce packets and some hot mustard and pretty much had the other vehicles loaded up by the time all the Wongs' and cousins and uncles showed up in three cars to convoy out of the area. They all said their farewells and set out for their destinations dodging a few crazy drivers but it wasn't too bad yet getting around on the back streets.

Hogan and Annie had put their leftover little boxes of Chinese dinners and the soft-shell crabs in a plastic sack with a few scoops of the meager ice that remained in the establishment and were grinning like Cheshire cats that they had found this bounty today. Not only did they get today's meal but also had gotten leftover Chinese takeout for tomorrow's gourmet dinner in one big lucky fell swoop.

"What's next on the agenda?" Annie asked feeling pretty good for the moment but still worried to death about what was predicted to be starting up in full force about 9 o'clock tonight. The dang phone lines were jammed which added to her stress but she knew her family at home were all pulling together to survive this catastrophe and they all knew she would be doing the same as best she could.

"I knew that question was coming and I have been thinking on it, you go lose the extra fish and such before the ice melts and I will start picking up any firewood I can find laying around here. In a day or so we won't be even able to find so much as a twig around here, I bet. Most likely we will be ending up busting up furniture to feed my little rocket stove. Oh yea, if you really like doing favors for those neighbors of yours tell them as soon as the water cuts off to stuff their toilets with rags or something if they can't find the outside access pipe to their building to clog up. When the sewage plant shuts down everything is going to start backing up and run them out of their apartments if they don't." Hogan said warning her of the unexpected mess everyone would have to face soon eventually depending on location and number of people pouring river water down their commode tanks trying to flush.

"Damn, I hadn't thought of that." Annie said looking like she was going to tear up as things just kept getting worse around here with no end in sight.

"This crap is for real isn't it, Hogan?" Annie said.

"Too real, far too damn real and it is just getting started, darlin." Hogan said giving her an impromptu hug and releasing her quickly before he became emotional also.

Folks were living on borrowed time in the hospitals, the nursing homes and many other places and would likely not make it another day past tonight if they were dependant on electricity, he thought with a shudder. It was just too hard and depressing to think about the upcoming misery in its hugeness and he just hoped these people had someone caring enough to be there for them in their last moments. Now on to the living and making sure he and Annie suffered as little as possible in their own circumstances.

"I will be back soon." Annie said and touched him on the shoulder to reassure that troubled look he wore before she walked off carrying her boxes full of perishable food treasures for the neighbors.

Hogan looked up at his apartment's balcony and cringed at the thought of having to cook dinner every day on it. Where else could he cook? On the range or in the kitchen sink with his rocket stove he guessed might work if the windows were open. But it was still going to be a chore trying to keep it somewhat secret as well as safe with all the food smells. No worries tonight or for at least a week anyway, people would be cooking what they had in their cupboards and freezers for awhile, but what then would it be like when everyone ran out of food?

Travel timing remained an important issue, when should they attempt getting out of here and where should they try to go to? He and Annie needed to focus and talk some more on the evolving situation and examine a lot of different options. The first thing they needed to discuss being the threat of a possible mega fire tonight engulfing the surrounding neighborhoods.

Now based on what he knew so far and what he had learned half listening to the radio on their trip to the shopping center was that he knew the power companies were turning the voltage off and that should mean hopefully the fire threat got greatly reduced. However, he didn't know just exactly how that would help, but he was grateful for it. The nuances of electrical power lines acting like antennas even without power flowing through them still concerned him though. This was pretty confusing to consider. Hell for that matter other than saying disconnect all small electronics and chargers and such the emergency broadcast system hadn't said diddly about if the solar storm generated EMP or geomagnetic pulses would be strong enough to affect car computer electronics or any other kind of circuitry.

Hogan decided he better take the contacts off the batteries of his and Annie's vehicles to help mitigate some damage hopefully. That chore might give him and her a bit of an edge maybe by keeping their transportation partly protected until the storm passed. He also needed to go wrap up his AM-FM radios in foil and better yet stick them in the microwave to shield them like a Faraday cage.

Hum, what else? Hogan pondered as he set about removing his battery cables and thinking about siphoning off some of his gasoline to store away from the vehicle but he didn't have a container. He had just filled his gas outboards tank as well as a 5 liter container yesterday for the fishing trip today that never happened so he forgot about that idea for now.

He just concerned himself with the present for now and aimlessly wandered around thinking while picking up twigs and sticks and such until Annie returned and told him mission accomplished and that everyone was happy with the unexpected bounty.

She also had a bit of advice she suggested they might try from one of her neighbor's who said they were cooking everything in their freezer regardless if the oven was switching on and off with the power surges and outright shutdowns. As the power companies shuttled their lines around getting ready for the big complete turn off at the electrical plants, people tried to save what little they could awaiting the inevitable freezer meltdowns as the grid went dark.

"That neighbor's idea makes sense as long you watch closely what's going on with the temperature I guess. Ovens will hold heat for awhile after they go off so it might be just a matter of guesstimating and trying not to open the oven door much, I figure. Let's go get ours started and try to make some jerky out of that beef we got."

Hogan said getting ready to go back to his apartment.

"How long are we going to be staying here in the apartment complex? You give it much more thought? The reason I am asking is that I got some more clothes back at my apartment I might need to bring over here." Annie asked.

"Hell, I don't know; I was going to talk to you some more on that. I am still worried about fires starting up and having to flee here. Let's go back to the apartment and discuss it in more detail. The first thing we need to talk about and decide on is the boats." Hogan said.

"What about them? Oh, you maybe mean going ahead and inflating them next time the power comes back on?" Annie asked.

"No, I don't really need to do that but it is something to consider. I don't need an 110v electrical outlet because my electrical air pump is battery operated. Remind me to be sure to shield that pump in some way or at least disconnect that big battery. It might be cool to go ahead and air up the boats and recharge the inflator if the electricity stays on long enough maybe. Tell you what no need to consider that this minute we still also have our manual air pumps as back up. We take us a prepping break and talk over lunch and as I am cooking them delicious crabs up." Hogan said helping Annie get her suitcase and a few other things out of her car and then carrying the stuff up the stairs.

"Do you really think everything is going to burn like you warned Mr. Wong it might back at the restaurant? " Annie asked after they got everything lugged up to the apartment.

"To tell you the truth I just don't know darling. I am kind of short on technical understanding and there are many variables. Will there be a bunch of fires? Yes I think there will be, will they drive us out of here and force us to flee by river? I don't know. Look here, Annie, at this bit of research I was doing for a paper on the 1859 Carrington event based on eyewitness accounts. You see nothing is cut and dry with these solar disturbances and geography as well as a few mysterious electrical things I don't know about come into play." Hogan said getting his laptop out and showing her a section of a university insight paper he had written relating to technology back in the day.

"When American Telegraph Company employees arrived at their Boston office at 8 a.m., they discovered it was impossible to transmit or receive dispatches. The atmosphere was so charged, however, that operators made an incredible discovery: They could unplug their batteries and still transmit messages to Portland, Maine, at 30- to 90-second intervals using only the auroral current. Messages still couldn't be sent as seamlessly as under normal conditions, but it was a useful workaround. By 10 a.m. the magnetic disturbance abated enough that stations reconnected their batteries, but transmissions were still affected for the rest of the morning."

"See these particular telegraph operators experienced mostly plasma phenomena while other operators in the US and around the World experienced various types of fires and equipment failure like this section speaks of." Hogan said tracing his finger down the page to point out some different data.

"On the night of August 28 as the first of two successive solar storms struck, E.W. Culgan, a telegraph manager in Pittsburgh, reported that the resulting currents flowing through the wires were so powerful that platinum contacts were in danger of melting and "streams of fire" were pouring forth from the circuits. In Washington, D.C., telegraph operator Frederick W. Royce was severely shocked as his forehead grazed a ground wire. According to a witness, an arc of fire jumped from Royce's head to the telegraphic equipment. Some telegraph stations that used chemicals to mark sheets reported that powerful surges caused telegraph paper to combust."

"Now I can show you other sections in this document that had some of the telegraph offices themselves catch on fire as well as adjoining buildings from the poles the telegraph wires were strung from but you get my drift about how unpredictable the effects of a Coronal Mass Ejection can be. Uncontrolled fires are my major concern tonight and how they might end up threatening us." Hogan said as he and Annie set about bugging into the apartment for the time being and getting the small wood fire started in the rocket stove to cook dinner.

"I wish you had a solar oven." Annie said as she watched Hogan getting things ready.

"I do! Well I take that back, I have got the makings of one to create a do it yourself one, anyway. We will work on that simple project maybe tomorrow; meantime let's get back to how I think things might play out for us in the coming days. You want me to tell you the best case or worst case scenario first?" Hogan said mixing up some prepackaged tempura batter he had in the house to dip the soft-shell crabs in.

"I guess give me worst case scenario first. Damn! Cooking oil! I forgot all about needing more cooking oil! That stuff will be like liquid gold now. Shoot, I could have traded those fish and shrimp and squids and such for some more cooking oil and maybe some canned goods! Oh well, no sense regretting a good deed having been done but it would have been easy at that time to borrow some oil in exchange for a fish to cook ours with." Annie fumed thinking she just missed the best barter situation she might have ever had.

"Dang, I didn't think of doing that either! My horse trading old soul must be snoozing! We sure missed ourselves a great opportunity to acquire some cooking oil, I suppose. But hey, no worries, we passed on the gift in the spirit it was given to us so what the hell? Maybe we will get some brownie points or good karma out of doing that." Hogan said wondering if that favor might come back to haunt them later.

"I can always go talk to them about trading for some oil in the future." Annie began before Hogan nixed the idea.

"No forget that. I don't want to be asking or having to bargain over anything with anybody in the future and I hope they don't ask me for anything of mine." Hogan said turning sour all of the sudden.

"Now ain't you being the turd in the punchbowl." Annie said rebuking his comment.

"Sorry Annie!" Hogan said not being able to not chuckle at the insult she had thrown in his direction.

"I just meant that I have a lot of reservations about how we are going to have to deal with the number of people that are living right next-door to us who will be asking me if I have got anything to eat soon. I don't think I can handle that very well. I think I have got too big of a heart to just say no for one thing and for another I know only of a few stages of mean to get them to leave us alone. When they start begging for food a situation can escalate quickly and violently if we chose the wrong action or reaction. I don't like anticipating seeing myself in a position where I can't share and have to run off someone begging, let alone the thought I might have to consider having a gun battle over a can of sardines as the insanity sets in." Hogan said a bit more openly than he wanted to be. He looked embarrassed that he would rather just wander around looking mean or hard in public and staying aloof rather than have others approach him in this chaos looking for some kind of help from him.

Hogan kind of figured it was safer for everyone that way. Otherwise, how did you know what stranger was a likeminded survivor or had criminal intents on his supplies? Hogan had some odd mental defensive systems that were directly attached to his trigger finger. Being a former military man, some would say he had no problem pulling a trigger on a situation or taking a life, but Hogan knew it was that constant judgment call to not pull it that made the soldier and everyone handled this kind of stress differently. He preferred avoidance and how best to avoid a situation like the one he was in now than to remove himself from the situation as much as he could?

"If the fires don't start threatening us around here later tonight and the smog from the burning city and chemical laden smoke doesn't get too bad over the coming days, I say we sit tight and leave from here in two or three weeks. We are going to drive out of here if we hear on the radio the roads are passable or could be the National Guard mobilizes and the Army clears the highways for truck traffic and we can get out that way. In the worst case scenario, I imagine that we are going to have to bug out and hide in the woods off the river somewhere and maybe run from brush and city fires the best we can. That's my plans in a nut shell." Hogan said trying to put a flexible timeline on their actions.

"Well, Hogan, you certainly didn't mince your words. I also see those as our only viable options unless a miracle happens and it looks like I can someway drive all the way home. I don't have the gas to even approach that so I will likely just follow you. Like you said, this crap is pretty unpredictable." Annie said making Hogan flinch at the thought of her attempting to be driving all that distance alone and also that he would lose his new friend and be left alone to face the terrors of this new world that would be unfolding all around them soon.

"I really hope you can get home to your family." Hogan said trying to act cheery for her but not really meaning it selfishly.

"Oh you're just being nice, I know it's a bit of a farfetched wish but I do have hope. Anything is possible as you said and maybe the states next to us won't be as hard hit. Hey maybe I will get to see that prepper shack of yours that you have been telling me all about and show me how you garden?" Annie said trying not to get in the dumps about a situation that probably couldn't be changed.

"Could be, we shall see. I figure we just bug in and stay inside as best we can. No reason for us to go out anywhere except maybe down to the river to draw water and that's it, well that and get rid of trash or use the latrine. Speaking of latrines it's about to get real funky nasty around here when the water stops for good. That could be if it stops entirely, there is just no telling if that electrical shutdown will help them restart the turbines again or not. I figure the water department has got enough fuel for the emergency generators to diesel power the pumps for a few weeks, if need be. The electrical outage shouldn't affect natural gas too much but then again won't be any fun around here if the gas mains somehow catch on fire. Anyway, if the water flows, the city flows; if the water stops, the city stops and the people have to leave, simple as that. Speaking of water flowing, I wonder what in the world the dam is going to be doing? This river gets kind of crazy with the water levels when the dam starts releasing water. Usually I refer to the dam's website for level schedules but I can't do that at the moment to get any news." Hogan said.

"That is a good question." Annie said pondering it.

"I say that they retain water in the reservoir so they can dump it over the turbines to restart the generators." Hogan said pondering it.

"Is that how they do it? Wouldn't they dump the water while not producing power and let the water build back up on its own since the pumps will be down?" Annie questioned.

"Well you could very well be right. I don't know much about how that thing works or their emergency plans for a disaster but I would say if you predict increase in fires you need more water so they would keep the reservoir full. Who knows? That could be a good thing because it will block a lot of that sewage and such that will be flowing into the river and polluting the hell out of everything." Hogan said not liking the sounds of the options they had going on.

"So how far down the river do you plan on going if we end up having to go with that mode of transport? I am guessing that there is going to be a lot of people migrating towards water around all those state parks and such down that way." Annie said.

"I figured the same; I have got me a hard to spot campsite all picked out upstream from the parks to hang out at for a bit. Its remote and being upstream I won't have to worry about all the pollution from the humans at the park washing downstream on me; course we got a whole city on the other side. People will be driven to seek out water to live; refugees will be on the move migrating towards any water source. I figure gas powered outboards as well as rowing and paddling craft will eventually bottleneck around the end of the kayak trail. I don't want to be there when everyone starts bugging out into the woods or gets stranded on the river bank somehow thinking they can make it just fishing. Somehow or another we got to find ourselves a way to portage and hopscotch around obstacles to more navigable waters and keep heading south. I see some likely options on this road map I got but that doesn't mean I know where rapids are etc." Hogan said trying to explain that the end of the rainbow was fraught with danger that he had yet to figure out how to get around.

"I have seen the devastation a thousand acre wildfire can cause so I understand your concerns about firestorms that may spin off to enflame neighborhoods. Have you thought about that there are a lot of clear areas and streets and stuff around us so maybe we won't have to rush out and get out onto the river just to escape the inferno? I do think though, Hogan, your idea of us hanging tight and waiting it out here and trying to drive out after the migration mayhem dies down is a pretty good one. With what supplies we have here on hand we could stay here for months bugged in if need be. A steady diet of beans and rice is going to suck but I will be damn grateful for it so excuse me when I complain later. What about the fish in the river, Hogan? I mean will they be safe for us to eat?" Annie asked thinking how they were going to augment their diet.

"Well, I hope we can still fish but if we see a big fish kill on the river that means a major sewage or factory chemical spill etc. is coming downstream and we don't eat any, otherwise I think it would be ok. I wouldn't suggest us making any sushi out of them, though." Hogan said with a dry laugh.

"So what is the bug out strategy on the boats? I mean I can inflate mine with air in about eight minutes but that's not something I care to be trying to be doing in the parking lot with smoke and ash flying in my direction." Annie declared imagining a horrific scene.

"Now that's a subject we got to put our prepper wits on. We should have a certain amount of prior warning that we need to move if a fire is approaching. I have been thinking on that some and have some observations. We will know tonight or by morning more on what the current fire situation is somewhat but we won't know for days its escalation, epicenter or its hottest burn direction. It's going to be difficult for us to judge though with all the smoke and haze I expect and who knows about changing wind directions. On the bright side, at least we don't have to worry ourselves any about airplanes falling out of the sky and crashing and burning all around us as everything in every airport is pretty much grounded nationwide. Keep in mind too, Annie, that they said we had a twelve hour warning but I know from experience that a coronal mass ejections effects can be here in less than an hour if a solar wind gets behind it. The governments most likely won't have a chance to tell anyone of the change in the storms arrival if that occurs so watch the skies for auroras. I say we just keep the boats put up and under wraps for now. I thought about filling up mine earlier and car-topping it but advertising that I have a boat could end up being problematic. Also I am worried if some idiot decides he is mad at me or the world for some reason and decides to stick a hole in it. It only takes me about ten minutes to inflate it anyway and I can't see not having sufficient warning but you never know and it is easy to misjudge the speed and direction of fire. Loading the boats and getting them down to the river is another story, we got to think about how to stage our supplies for that." Hogan said as he dropped each battered soft shell crab into the hot oil and watched them sizzle.

"YUM! That looks and smells so good!" Annie said smiling and looked around the complex at other people starting their own dinners on BBQ grills and such.

"There are still a lot of cars missing out of the parking lot, Hogan. Do you think they are trying to leave the city?" Annie said speculating.

"I hate to say it but I hope so. The fewer people that will be remaining around us the better I like it but they could be anywhere. People could be stuck at work shutting crap down, they can be trying to buy food and water, some might be out of town etc. I guess we will know tonight when everyone should be home if they have any sense at all. Anyone stuck in traffic might end up walking home back here after a few days, that is if the cars still work. I am really worried about that particular major piece of hell occurring. Most likely vehicles will remain operational but not a lot is known about very high magnitude solar flares effects on cars electronics. If the computer chips do fry and transportation stops, we will be living here for a long time to come, I think." Hogan said flipping the crabs to cook the other side.

"I wish we could have these on toast but I am glad you still got a loaf of fresh bread. Are you going to try to make bread with all that flour you got?" Annie asked.

"I could maybe make something passable for a loaf of bread in a Dutch oven if I had the wood fuel needed to do it but I probably won't bother. Ha! If we end up going to the woods you are going to learn a new definition for a bread stick. That's going to be meaning dough wrapped around a stick and baked over coals! Oh and shovel cakes when I make pancakes on my entrenching tool over a campfire. Ha! Ha!" Hogan said while transferring his fried sea delicacies to a plate for a quick drain on paper towels before slapping one on a couple pieces of bread and nothing else and handing the sandwich to Annie.

"Wow I have died and gone to heaven! You can cook Hogan!" Annie said after the first bite and then the two munched their lunch and said little else until every morsel was gone.

"That was some fine eating and we still have some Chinese leftovers and all that meat half cooking in the oven. I guess we get to be gluttons before we will get to be starving!" Annie said rubbing her tummy.

"You got that right! It might be a bad way to get our stomachs into condition for lean times but if you look at it historically speaking our bodies were kind of made to do that. Indigenous peoples would go through periods of no game to hunt and subsist on roots and such and then someone kills something like a buffalo and everyone gorges for awhile until the cycle starts again." Hogan said eying the whiskey bottle but knowing he ought to be doing something more productive but what that something was he didn't have a clue at the moment and there was nothing to do but to wait.

"Let's go back to my house and get all my pots and pans brought over here to fill up with water. You know what? If there is any water pressure to speak of I think I'll wash out the trash cans and fill them up too." Annie said finding something more useful to do than start a hurricane party.

"I wish you hadn't told your neighbors you were leaving." Hogan said spoiling the upbeat mood.

"Why not? What's wrong with that? You didn't say a word about me saying not doing that when I mentioned it." Annie said concerned.

"Well I just started thinking this whole grid down thing out a bit further. From now on everybody will be watching everybody else's comings and goings. I don't think most people have the capability or knowledge to break into one of these steel door apartment units by themselves but it only takes a little determination and the right tools and you can get in. People will be looking for units that appear vacant or unattended to break into and look for supplies. Hey, have you seen our maintenance guys or manager anywhere today?" Hogan asked.

"Uh no, what do you want them for?" Annie asked.

"I think it might cost us that last hundred bucks you got to find out." Hogan said deciding just one more drink wouldn't hurt anything and heading for the bottle with the objecting Annie following him.

"But that's all the money we got left in the world and you know we will never probably see a bank open a door again maybe in our lifetime." Annie said demanding he stop what he was doing and talk to her.

"Chill out, you are going to like this idea and most likely I won't even need to use your money. I will get you some gold maybe to replace it soon if I do end up having to use it. Give me a minute to think this thing out and you can fuss at me for stealing a few ice cubes because I am going to have me a cold drink while I still can." Hogan said going over to the dining room table and putting on his shoulder rig holster again.

"That looks like you're expecting trouble! What's up? Where are you going?" Annie said pointedly.

"No, Annie, this looks like I am thinking about causing some of my own trouble if need be, but don't worry. This mad monkey has a plan." Hogan said and then went to his dresser drawer and strapped onto his belt a spare small sheath knife he wore in State Parks when they had a Bowie knife ban that prevented him from carrying a bigger blade.

"Where you do plan on going? You haven't said yet. Do I need to be strapping on gear too?" Annie said a bit flustered that Hogan wasn't talking enough and instead flitting around his apartment grabbing bits of this and that and adding to his pockets.

"You might say that I am going foraging for a fugitive to help us out getting something." Hogan said with a grin enjoying tormenting his friend Annie just a bit more. It was usually her that could set Hogan up for a fall and a funny remark but he was in his own when it came to preparedness points to ponder and dangle at her strong curiosity. He enjoyed playing with her dangling tid bits of preparedness and survival tricks at her while she in response acted like a cat that couldn't resist or pass up a bit of yarn to bat around.

"What is the easiest way to break into a vacant apartment for supplies, would you say little Miss Annie?" Hogan said with a mock snide look.

"There is a trick to this! I know there is and I know you!" Annie said studying the smirk Hogan was trying to not show.

"How can that be a trick question? Ok, I will phrase it another way. What is the least path of resistance to get into one of these apartments?" Hogan said sipping his drink and then putting it down as an idea came to mind to exchange the shirt he was wearing over his shoulder rig and t shirt for an olive drab fishing vest with a concealed carry holster built in. He removed his shoulder rig and put the pistol in the vests inside pocket.

"I guess I would break a window or jimmy a patio door." Annie said confident in her response.

"Nernt! Wrong answer!" Hogan said making a buzzer like noise.

"You are on the right track though both of those ideas would work easier than trying the front door. The answer that I wanted you to say was using a freaking key to open the door. I bet you know who has the master keys for everything around here. Like you said there are lots of people leaving and seemingly for the moment not making it back home etc. Pretty soon I am sure that even if it's nothing but a roll of toilet paper there is going to be something in those empty apartments in a week or two we and a lot of others want. So once everyone who is watching and wondering about those empty units and what they might contain they will start considering breaking and entering them for survival sake if nothing else. So you think in order to get a hold of some supplies do you think they might team up with others to do just that?" Hogan said letting out some more yarn.

"Then they either break in as a group or use a key if they have one?" Annie said searching his face for any more clues to this frustrating game.

"Exactly! So bottom floor units might get their patio windows smashed one night or somebody will be hunting for the resident manager for a key and maybe offering to share the wealth with him for unlocking the door. But she ain't going to be there, she will be the fugitive everyone is cussing for leaving the property and taking the keys with her. Now if I can either talk or scare her into seeing things my way and get her to move upstairs in that empty apartment over me, we might have some new angles to work off of. I bet she already knows which apartment belongs to someone out of town on business or vacation. If I can get her on my side and under my protection as it were we might be able to go "shopping" right now and get her and ourselves established with a lot more canned goods than we have now." Hogan said thinking that people have been known to tell their landlord they would be away for a period of time.

Hey first come first serve when it comes to survival supplies, Hogan thought. Someone was going to get those empty apartment supplies eventually and he saw nothing wrong with using a little influence to stack the deck on his side to insure his survival and help someone else. A bit immoral maybe he thought if it somehow turned out a person managed to make it back here only to find their pantry totally empty, he couldn't live with himself if that happened. Well maybe he could keep an eye on the places and sneak some food back to them if he saw someone appear out of nowhere but he would jump that hurdle when he encountered it.

"So you are going to try to kidnap the apartment manager? Well that's an exaggeration but I wouldn't put it past you to scare her to death with looter zombie stories. What will the neighbors say if they see her moving over here?" Annie asked not so sure this was a good idea and somehow might expose them to even more danger.

"There is a young couple who are living across from that apartment. I don't know them personally but I do see them occasionally and I think they are the type of people that can most likely be convinced to keep their mouths closed once they find out the manager is now living across from them for their own safety if nothing else. Damn, I wish people would speak to each other more these days. Right now I am wishing I had talked to all the neighbors around here some rather than just giving the occasional nod at them as we come and go. Anyway, I am going to try to gain access to the keys to this little kingdom before somebody else thinks of the same notion and beats me to it." Hogan said mischievously.

"I sort of see where you are going with this crazy plan. You want to stockpile that apartment over us with whatever we can find in vacant apartments and install the manger up there correct? I can understand that reasoning but I can also see some dangers in it we need to discuss. I still can't however figure out what you need my hundred bucks for?" Annie said holding the bill up between two fingers.

"Thanks." Hogan said reaching over and snagging it

"I doubt I will need it now that I am talking this little nefarious plot through but I was thinking I might want to borrow a ladder I would forget to return from the maintenance guys, if I can find them. They might need some palm greasing but I need me a ladder if the manager balks to get easier access to balconies I might want to explore someday. I am also betting they might have some plywood in the maintenance shed to cover up broken windows and such that they might sell me so I can fortify and secure my place a bit." Hogan said putting the bill far down in his shirt pocket for ready access to pull out at just the right point in an anticipated negotiation.

"So are you going over there and trying to convince her your' Billy Badass that can save the day and protect her from the mutant ninja biker hordes that already have her name on a list to visit or are you going to be civil about it? Maybe I should come with you." Annie began advising before Hogan cut her off saying he wasn't going to fear monger much, just show the woman the error in her ways of thinking should she disagree with his proposition.

" Now Annie I think as a someone that alleges to be a so called professional licensed professional in adverting disasters and "experienced in emergency management" I can maybe sway her into helping us out a little bit if we have offered to help her out some and increase her chances of getting through this calamity without extra drama. I want to feel her out good first though. I don't know that woman at all except to say hi and from when I signed the lease months ago though. I doubt she even owns a gun for personal protection and I don't think she has even considered yet how many people might be coming to her apartment or office real soon wanting those keys for any other reason but a lockout. Either way, it is time for me to do a better more informed meet and greet. I am just going to go have a friendly visit and make nice for now and see about that ladder and plyboard, I think. I will start with innocent normal resident inquiries like preparing my house for winter so the pipes don't bust in a freeze if I was going somewhere and If maintenance is around I will advise them I want to know about any cutoff valves or access holes for sewage lines maybe to get ready for the backed up puking toilet sewage crisis that may happen." Hogan said looking forward to this bit of psychological warfare and influence gathering he was going to attempt before adding he would see her back here or at her apartment shortly while she saw to collecting more water and containers from her apartment.

Hogan walked down to the office but nobody was there. "Dang it, I hate when a plan doesn't come together!" He fumed while looking around for any kind of activity.

There used to be a little note card in a frame on the door listing the maintenance and managers phone numbers as well as the resident managers apartment number but it was gone. No cars were located in the reserved parking places so he walked across the complex to the maintenance shed and it was locked up and nobody was around there either.

"Seems that I can't win for losing today!" Hogan muttered to himself considering visiting a few places with "Moe" one dark night referring to his multi tool axe from Schrade that he considered his can opener for prying open things that needed to be seen or explored more.

Lighter than a giant crowbar and concealable on your person or a shoulder bag if you stopped to figure it out, it was his go to "master key" in times of trouble like this to gain access or rescue someone. Resistance and security was not a word that would trouble gaining entry one way or another with that tool to most everything he might need if the coast was clear...

He scanned the area to see if people were observing his interest in the possibly now abandoned vacant steel building. The few people he observed from his vantage point looked like they were busy loading up cars to go somewhere soon which made Hogan smile, but other thoughts soon put a frown on his face as he immediately started pondering their fates.

Hogan guessed many tenants would be attempting to journey towards relatives and families to ride this thing out in the countryside or somewhere else safer while still others might have a different agenda unbeknownst to him and were hurrying also to get to parts unknown. He wondered if the apartment manager might have gone on such a mysterious mission and how long it would be before the offsite living maintenance crew decided to think about coming here to salvage things they thought they might need.

He didn't want to be accused of thievery or taking advantage of a situation before the breakdown had even started good and his proposed actions wouldn't look like blatant looting and advantage taking that could cause him some problems now or later.

A lot of people could be observed still idly sitting on their balconies apparently in shock in reaction to what was transpiring as the modern world started to end. It was spooky; the whole area seemed strangely quiet somehow. The recognition of the final radio messages that had aired must have begun to sink in that everyone was on their own now and would remain that way for a long time to come.

It was unnatural, it was more than unnerving for anyone to attempt to wrap their head around that the lights wouldn't be coming back on tomorrow or the next day for a long time to come. The people were flat out told that they would be on their own for a month or more until the government could regroup and try to send its citizens some aid. Most people in this privileged society we live in could not even begin to conceive that they were officially on their own from now on with no state or federal safety nets to save their soon to be sorry scrawny butts from starvation.

This just couldn't happen in this politically correct and entitlement world they were used to living in. Oh some already were wasting their time organizing riots so they could flash rob stores and do a bit of looting because the "man" wasn't going to take care of them any more under their self assumed rights regarding color or gender or whatever.

Yes the cops and the National Guard would try to prevent such actions for a day or so before their families became more important to them than serving undesirable elements needs to have to get hit on the head to cease being a fool before their own families protection became more important and they just didn't show up for work one day.

"But how long will that take?" Not too long Hogan figured.

You will have enough no shows and not reporting for roll call or drill because the communications systems were down but you would also have an increasingly aware first responder group that said screw it under these conditions and let the idiots go ahead and burn their own neighborhoods down in protest for things they couldn't or wouldn't comprehend as society without media to fan the flames would be obviously not present to scapegoat them and their actions to restore order.

Bad folks would end up having bad endings and Hogan didn't care too much about them at the moment other than they were the ones that wouldn't let sane society cope. Well not in America, anyway. He had often marveled at the Japanese who were well known for their patience and community spirit in standing in long lines for hours patiently waiting their turn to get into a store after a tsunami or earthquake devastated a township.

Those people could do all the self righteous BS posturing and burning establishments they wanted to instead of helping each other survive as a community. Most wouldn't get it anyway that they no longer had a camera to scream obscenities at that another race or religion wasn't helping them or gifting them for being different anyway and that it was in some way their whiteness maybe fault they had burned their own houses and stores down as they usually did. He didn't care about these fringe elements usually found in the disturbed mental ghettos of America and he didn't blame not a one of the people or soldiers and policemen of every race and religious denomination that wasn't going to show up in a couple days to say their food stamps and welfare checks didn't work anymore when nothing else in more affluent areas did either.

Disasters segregate people because like wants to be with like and people that share the same values get along fine no matter what their race or religion are as long as they have a moral compass. Yes later on in a disaster the old prejudices arrive but mostly folks in general should be beyond that. Don't start picking an old worn out scab and saying you are special in some way or another needing special treatment when it is only the basic character of a person that equates wrong or right and socially morally principled to not create havoc.

The few conversations Hogan had managed to overhear seemed to be more hushed than conversational and people stared at him watchful and apprehensive.

"It isn't me you need to worry about unless you mess with me." Hogan thought with a scowl.

All these people who didn't have a clue what to do next would soon be burdening others instead of coming together as a community to try to survive.

Hogan wasn't going to get himself killed trying to help them, he was going to be as self centered as they were and if push came to shove he would either survive or try to go down in style.

3

Perceptions And Foreboding

Day two of the disaster had nature and her dazzling lights putting on a bit of a show by weaving warped pallets of colors into the smoke and the haze hanging over the city and countryside. In the early morning hours hues of green and yellow spread their tendrils ever skyward mixing with the fiery red.

Cars still worked and operated as normal as of 9 am this morning. Well that was the time when Hogan and Annie saw one pull out of the parking lot and leave the apartment building next to them. That was before the blood red glow started up again rising from the horizon like some big blood red moon ready to engulf the world. One odd thing that occurred really startled them and this was when a street light suddenly glowed momentarily and then went out after a few seconds. Hogan had seen a couple of the post mounted lights do that spluttering thing afterwards and he could still be heard asking strangers as he was wandering up to the main road to see if any car traffic or breakdowns were occurring, if they had seen any kind of phenomenon like that going on this morning.

One person had said tthat he smoke alarms in his building went off for a second or two but they figured that it was the smoke in the air that had caused it. One said the car alarms in the parking lot got crazy for a minute. Hogan was very tempted to ask them to go try to start their cars but didn't. That knowledge he speculated was an awful rusty double edged sword to be possessing right about now.

Ignorance is bliss they say. Hogan kind of felt like that saying "Wow I saw a street light flicker on this morning! Isn't that weird they can do that with no electricity supposedly in the lines?" to a stranger that acknowledged his hello. Hogan thought this was a pretty good opening line to gather info with but it didn't work too well. People were scared right now and seemed pretty stand offish enough as it was without him saying he saw lights when there weren't any supposedly possible. People just didn't want to be bothered about stopping and talking about anything at all. There loss Hogan figured.

He didn't quite feel like saying anything to them either by this time. Particularly telling them things like "Hey by the way there is a huge chance your cars won't start pretty soon! Have you tried starting yours lately? Yea right, folks would be looking at him wondering if he were crazy or be asking him what they could do about it maybe if they didn't start. That's a damned if you do damned if you don't proposition all the way around to consider.

If he said " Hey I disconnected my battery cables in hopes my car computer doesn't fry some folks would be like "Well the radio didn't say anything about doing that" to the inevitable question of how did he know that bit of info and did he think that trick would help any, to which that answer right or wrong could get him into lots of trouble.

No, he decided right now his best course of action was to keep his head down and his mouth shut. Generally speaking if someone spoke to him he said little of his own personal knowledge of solar storms and chose to go with the flow concerning conversations with the unknowing and unprepared neighbors.

If they didn't know anything, then he didn't know anything either. He told Annie for them it was best to just play "Gray Man." It was watch, wait and see time for them to just blend in with the crowd and not stand out in anyway.

Hogan knew an odd thing that most folks didn't know or failed to take into account about a disaster like a hurricane. The day after one occurs; people in the stricken area generally are at their best in terms of being kind and helping each other out.

They want to help their neighbors, they like greeting a stranger warmly and they tend to get along with the community at large by sharing the experience of surviving the same hardships. This is because they understand or could anticipate a common core of problems they themselves would have to bear with everyone else trying to get through a calamity.

Now this particular disaster was different to consider just how people were going to act in the coming days. People knew help wasn't going to be coming anytime soon. The radio gave a laughable estimate of hope that people might have to wait up to five weeks in cities to receive coordinated Federal aid, but it would be limited in scope because this was a nationwide event that over taxed resources.

After the President declared a National Emergency and Martial Law both dang near in the same sentence on the radio, he said he was convening the Congress of Governors in one week in Washington D.C. This meeting was to be held after the effects of the Solar Storm on air travel was suspected to cease and he explained that all National Guard Units were Federalized and for all enlisted personnel and reserves to find their way to their respective home units and armories.

Travel restrictions would be announced, the federalization of the national electrical grid, oil refineries, all trains and commerce transportation facilities as well as the appointment of two agricultural czars for increasing the national stockpile of grains and dairy products and the presidents list went on.

Hogan told Annie that March 23rd should be remembered as "Evoke" day because he had heard the word used so much today on the radio. Evoke this and evoke that. Some speaker with a title he had never heard of would say that of according to this article or that section or paragraph of the emergency powers acts, that they were evoking their special governmental control for the duration of this declared state of emergency and poof! No more private ownership, no more Constitutional rights, no habeas corpus!

Now Mr. Pres and all the state and local governments have all got these but "If" or "when" rules that say that they alone know what is best for everyone in a emergency. They dictate that normal rules of governance get superseded by their executive will and the emergency declaration laws that they continue to expand and write for themselves.

Under extraneous conditions they have the power not only to tax but confiscate wealth and goods. They can even regulate the rationing of toilet paper. That is why America has been in a legal perpetual state of emergency for so long, that's how they qualify their right to tax your income, toy with implementing the draft etc.

What the National Emergencies Act does is act like a little bright glowing toggle switch, and when the president flips it, he gets new powers. Prang! Now I have super powers to do what I want, look at me! Like he doesn't have enough authority already! Hogan sighed.

It's like a magic wand and he is the only one that can wave it and there are very few constraints about how he turns the magic on...

Those emergencies at the federal level, the ones declared by the president by proclamation or executive order, give the president extraordinary powers — to seize property, call up the National

Guard and hire and fire military officers at will. That's right, he is commander and chief.

Since 1976, when Congress passed the National Emergencies Act, presidents have declared at least 53 states of emergency — not counting disaster declarations for events such as tornadoes and floods, according to a USA TODAY review of presidential documents. Most of those emergencies remain in effect to this day.

Even as Congress has delegated emergency powers to the president, it has provided almost no oversight. The 1976 law requires each house of Congress to meet within six months of an emergency to vote it up or down. That's never happened. I wonder how everyone managed to overlook this fact so many times?

Hogan in his mind knew about this power grab and he knew once people or politicians got a taste of it they didn't like to give it back. Now Hogan had never written a plan on surviving government usurpation of powers or insurrection or anything close to that. It was probably written somewhere it was illegal to do that.

He was however publically out spoken in his patriotic constitutionalist views, he had put his time in the military and he had helped more people plan for and survive disasters than most, in other words he had served his country well.

However his governmental dealings were based on avoidance of bureaucratic BS not engagement. He wanted to be far away from the closely regulated life he saw coming. The current curfews and travel restrictions that were being imposed now under martial law would look like the good old times to what he foresaw as the old school guard tried to impose its militaristic will on the citizens as this disaster developed.

About the only plausible plan the government could use to reconstruct would come from its military arm, not FEMA and its minions. The U.S. military has practice at this destroyed city rebuilding, lots of very "RECENT" practice gained from the declared/undeclared wars in the Middle East and playing with Russia in the Crimea and beyond.

The Russians were talented in imposing their will by shutting off fuel oil, gas, food, electricity you name it if they wanted to reel in one of their more belligerent outlying states or NATO countries. They were practiced at enforcing their will on citizens and enemies under war conditions also.

"The world has been at war many times and rebuilding society always happens in one way or another so why not now?" Hogan had mused previously regarding the event that he was experiencing now. He in tried to contemplate a

fictional future for his preparedness clients to get back on their feet after a major disastrous event . Cities had been firebombed to hell and back, nuclear bombs dropped you name it and business and population centers came back. So why would it be so hard to conceive that the military already had a reconstruction plan for what was going on now?

This wasn't a hard task at all to speculate on unless you tried to figure out your place in the scheme of things. How far back in the ration line you would stand and that was if there were any rations to be given out. People don't like to know that they were just a number, a subtractable or addable number that had no individual bearing on the outcome of the "plan." How people acted when they received the aid as well as if the populace looked at you as a benefactor or occupier helped or hindered actions.

Just what level of misery it took to for you to get classified as a survivor, refugee, displaced person or whatever also indicated what camp conditions would be like if you ended up in a relief center.

A Eureka moment suddenly came to Hogan. A brilliant clarity of mind you might say touched him based solely on his primal instincts versus his educated mind, but you would be wrong. Where do

I want to stand and be classified as in this world right now he thought? If I don't matter I want to stand in the middle where I won't be counted and remain unnoticed, he said to himself. Not on this side, not on that side, just a free man living life as best he could. He smiled at his simple condition in life now and the choices he could make for himself, by himself. He wanted to get away from everything, away from this place and live unnoticed.

Hogan thought of his friends Lori and Sam who had really got him into this river camping idea by them introducing him to a portable survival trailer, bug out recreation boat thing a year or so back.

Hogan had met Sam at an annual camping meet in Florida called "Preppers On the Beach" and had been amazed you might say as well as become pretty much infatuated with the idea of the marvelous boat Sam had brought there. It was called a Tetra Pod Trailer. Why that marvelous thing was the coolest slickest idea since sliced bread in Hogan's opinion.

It was a survival trailer that could fold out and turn into a boat! How cool was that? But the neatest concept to it was how Sam had integrated it into his and Lori's lifestyle.

Sam was the creatively inspired survivalist one that had pointed out to Hogan the joys a prepper could have living what he called the "lifestyle" of practicing preparedness recreation boating. Not only did you get to enjoy normal fishing and camping around lakes and rivers, you also had the opportunity of interacting with a myriad of like minded people sharing skills and pleasurable company in the outdoors.

Old Sam in Hogan's mind had always been his favorite prepper par excellent for a number of reasons, mostly because it seemed the guy could always adapt to the ever changing tides of fate he was exposed to and bounce back as a winner or master of something new.

Sam had told him his ingenious master plans for survival and experiences from everything from truck gardening when he lost a job to how to live in the woods next to a lake for an extended stay and catch a fish on a twig. (Sam didn't mean using a twig as a fishing pole neither as you might think. He meant using a thumbnail length piece of stick sharpened on each end as a hook to catch a fish! (Go look up a fish gorge on Google if you don't know this trick.)

When Sam was asked what he was going to do, or where he was going to go when SHTF, he always just said he was going to "Check Out Of Society." Nothing more, just that he was going to drop out and live life best as he could.

"He told me that he was going to grab the girl, the gear and the grub and hightail it to a place not a bunch of people knew about and be a beach bum." Hogan said grinning to himself remembering fondly the man sharing bits of woods lore with him over a cold one.

"Did he actually tell you where he was going to try to get to or did he keep big secrets to himself also?" Annie said playfully hinting she wanted to know more about Hogan's secret bug out location on the river..

"Maybe he did try to keep some secrets from me. I don't really know if he had a specific place in mind that he was going to or not. They travelled around a lot of northwest Florida. He just said he was heading for Florida's Forgotten Coast and we talked about a few areas in general but nothing specific." Hogan said pondering where exactly Sam had talked the most about above other places.

"Oh I have been to a few nice spots in north west Florida when I visited on vacation. It is absolutely gorgeous down there! Didn't you say this river ran in that direction?" Annie said excitedly.

"Yes you are correct; the river does go that way. There are a couple ways you can get there by water but it isn't a clear shot all the way straight through. I will show you on the map later a couple places we can put a boat in at that can get us on a hundred or so miles of open water to travel down and end up coming out right into the bay." Hogan said eying the two pillowcases of canned goods Annie had brought over and dropped next to the couch.

"Do you want me to put those cans up in your cabinets?" It won't take me a minute." Annie said thinking that since she was moving in here semi permanently they may as well get the food situation sorted out.

"Not just yet. Matter of fact I was trying to decide if I needed to bag mine up to be ready for a quick getaway. I still have uncontrolled fires on the brain and that huge drop in water pressure isn't helping that feeling any. I know I need to get my clothes together if I need to sky out of here though. Come on and follow me to the bedroom while I start getting those sorted and we can talk about what to do with the food." Hogan said heading down the short hallway.

"I probably need for you to help me bring some more clothes and other stuff over here from my apartment if you plan on bugging in here for awhile, but maybe not. I got the car crammed full of clothes that I won't probably be wearing anytime soon anyway." Annie replied.

"Did you grab all your winter stuff?" Hogan asked starting to stuff his heavy weight field jacket along with a wool OD green sweater into an old military duffle bag.

"No I don't have any winter stuff to load. I didn't think I needed anything for awhile when I moved here and I was either going to get my winter clothes sent to me or go home before Thanksgiving and pick them up. I am going to be kind of in trouble aren't I Hogan come the fall?" Annie said regretting that she only had a lightweight jacket in her bug out gear and little else for the season of winter.

"Not necessarily, I don't have any wool skirts or girly winter hats with me but I have stuff you can wear. I have even more clothes and stuff in Alabama if we ever we get there for you to dig through so you will be ok." Hogan said going to his chest of drawers and getting his gloves and scarf and such.

"Don't say "if we ever" like there is any question of us not making it. I thought that was the big plan. We wait it out here and then we drive out when the roads clear." Annie said studying him.

"Oh that is my plan alright. I am just not nearly as hopeful as you are that the cars are going to remain working. I know supposedly the biggest geomagnetic storm pressure hit last night but we got today's incoming solar storm to contend with and whatever effects both of them cause for days communication wise. We will probably be on the receiving end of charged particles I am guessing for at least a week but they will be mild, not that it matters." Hogan said estimating when the major damage and threats would be occurring the most, well on this side of the planet anyway.

"I guess no one will know what's happening for at least a week then. I mean even though the emergency broadcast system is hardened for that type of EMP (Electromagnetic Pulse), if we can't get a transmitted signal it will be a radio blackout. That's if an unshielded radio still works and didn't get its circuitry fried." Annie added glad that theirs were safely residing in a makeshift faraday cage.

"Yea it's not like the government will be delivering us the Sunday newspaper telling us what's going on. I wish I had thought to bring my old rotary phone from prepper shack up here. Landlines will be working for the phone company mostly I imagine. I know the old system we had before they got into fiber optics was made to resist nuclear EMP but I don't know how much the upgrades will affect things." Hogan said regretting he only had an electrical nonworking phone.

"Hey what happens if I plug that phone into my portable car jumper? That's the ticket I bet that might work and Annie can get a call out to her family maybe." Hogan mused.

"I have an old phone that works when the powers out at home. Most people don't know there is a small amount of electricity on those lines even when the powers out. I wonder if they will shut that off low voltage off also. Do you know Hogan?" Annie asked.

"Good question! Want to find out? Oh crap!" I just thought of something. Hogan said jumping up and heading for the door.

"What's the matter Hogan?" Annie asked worriedly.

"I like an idiot left my jump starter in the back of my van." Hogan said rushing out to get it and mentally cursing himself for forgetting it.

"Oh hell!" Annie exclaimed as she followed him out.

Hogan unlocked the hatch on his van and fiddled with the jump starter once he located it and was rewarded with the loud sound of the air compressor going on.

"Yay!" They both giggled at one another as he immediately shut it down and removed it to carry back inside.

As he was locking his van back with his key he brought up an interesting point to Annie's question about "what happens to electronic locks on a car during a solar storm."

"I love talking to you Annie! You ask all the right questions that I haven't thought of yet. Now I have never seen any data on that electronic lock theory thing but I am guessing they stay locked. I remember they came out with a Corvette or something awhile back and the thing didn't have any manual release locks on it. You had a special place on the outside of the vehicle with battery contacts accessible for connecting a battery to in order to release the locks if the battery went out on it. They finally fixed that stupid idea after a few people got locked inside their cars and the company spent a lot of money informing first responders to just hook some jumper cables to them instead of tearing up the car. " Hogan said thinking it was a very good question as to whether or not cars would magically open once their circuits were fried.

"Wow I am glad that people won't necessarily get locked in their cars if the sun fries their computers. Be bad enough to be going 70 miles an hour down the road when your power steering gives out after the engine dies. If you lived through that and then found yourself unable to get out of the car it could be really bad. What do you think will happen to car computers in general, Hogan? I mean if the solar storm is powerful enough to melt their circuits, wouldn't the car catch fire?" Annie asked grateful she had someone like Hogan around to answer all these odd questions they needed to be concerned with.

"There you go again, great question! Let me refer back to the car locks or electronic locks in general because you got me to thinking about garage door openers and such. I say the wires melt so quickly that they can't start a fire most times and the lock remains closed but unencumbered to be unlocked manually. Let me explain what I mean by that. They use high temperature plastics in those things that tend to melt more than flame depending on temperature. The wires themselves or their connections will melt long before the box they are in so the surge of power stops. So an electronic lock as soon as it has negative bias to it will release whatever physically locks the lock and that's the end of it. A physical action like flicking a lever or pulling a button will override that and release it. I can't see any melting components interfering with that operation but you never know. Now car computers are another thing, every modern car today baffles me and whether a certain model has theirs inside or outside the firewall I can't even tell you that. I can tell you that from now on we are going to ride with the windows part way down because I don't want to be driving along and get stuck smelling acrid electrical smoke if the computer does decide to melt down or a stray stream of geomagnetic energy decides it doesn't like my radio antennae." Hogan said not too keen about driving around anywhere for awhile.

"Good answer, I suppose all those digital gas pumps have some kind of failsafe mechanism in them don't you think Hogan?" Annie said looking even more alarmed when Hogan evidently didn't have a ready answer for that.

"Dang I hope so, seems like they would. I really don't know though. If there is no electricity to pump the liquid fuel then I think the danger of fire is negligible. On the other hand you got us back to thinking on the lock question. The old mechanical gas pumps always had some fuel left in the hoses you could get even after you shut the pumps counter down. I think these modern ones do too but it won't give it to you before you start fueling. Remind me I need to check a shutdown fuel pump for gas in the hose just for the hell of it." Hogan advised.

"Looks like the gym rats are having themselves quite a barbecue." Annie said looking over at the corner of the next building and referring to a couple of over large weightlifters and their friends evidently having a use-up-the-freezer cookout.

"Leave it to me to have the incredible Hulk along with his hulksters to be living next to us during the apocalypse." Hogan said caught a little off guard by the five very large muscular tank top wearing fitness freaks laughing and having themselves a party around an expensive propane grill.

"I don't know why it is you dislike them folks so much, Hogan. I talked to the biggest one once and he seemed pretty nice." Annie started to object.

"You never been around when they have a football watching party or they come in the bar wanting to change the TV station. All the noises they make remind me of a pep rally for the Planet of The Apes." Hogan said not to be put off about his opinion of the boisterous over developed mutants in his mind's eye.

"You are just jealous your arms aren't that big." Annie said knowing she was going to get a rise out of Hogan by kidding him that way.

"They can be big as a house for all I care. I wonder where Misses Hulk is at. I saw her in a bikini once down at the pool and her dang arms are bigger than mine! I ain't a fan of that type of woman as you know and she takes that physical fitness body building to extremes. I think she got even more buff as they call it the last few months. Why her chest is so flat looking and distorted now I almost got caught scrutinizing her crotch to see if she was one of those Atlanta a he/ she's that are hard to recognize after I got done freaking out about studying her big butt before she stood up and turned around." Hogan said watching the athletes over at the other apartment joking with each other like they didn't have a care in the world and this was just another big hurricane party to them.

"I hope that is not all the food they have got." Hogan remarked.

"I sure wouldn't want to be the one to tangle with none of them over a can of food. Do you think they will be a problem, Hogan?" Annie asked now looking at them in another light.

"Me neither, but a .45 slug could settle any possible disputes with them from my end. I wonder if those boys are into guns or not. I don't see anyone carrying one off hand, do you?" Hogan asked looking them over more closely.

"I don't see any open carry pistols on them and I doubt they are concealing much with those shorts they got on. Are we going back in the apartment to try out that jump starter or hanging out here?" Annie asked.

"We will go back in shortly. I bet them boys have enough protein shakes and vitamins stored up to last them a month or two." Hogan whispered and then waved to the men who evidently noticed Hogan and Annie studying them.

Annie waved back also and they both politely declined an offer to participate in the cook out from one of the younger ones.

"See, they aren't so bad." Annie said in a low tone as Hogan decided to go back in.

"That remains to be seen. Annie that biggest lump has got to be on steroids or something. I wonder what steroid withdrawal does to someone. I know taking them can make you have violent outbursts as well as shrink your nuts they say but I don't know if anything happens when you try to come off of them." Hogan said leaving it to Annie to advise him the answer on that one.

"I don't know, I knew about that testosterone aggression thing but I never heard of that odd medical fact you just mentioned. Does it really? I mean you know? Shrink things?" Annie asked.

"That's what they say, can't imagine why a man would trade his virility for muscle mass but some do I guess. That was what they said when all that info come out a long time ago of the necessity to test Russian Olympic athletes as well as ours but I don't know. I also heard about it because some of those gyms have a black-market business in human growth hormones and such too. They are going to be getting hungry like everyone else though soon enough, protein shakes or not so I wouldn't be opening any doors for them if they come knocking to visit if you know what I mean." Hogan said pointedly.

"Point taken, anyone of them could force themselves in the door pretty easily if they wanted to, I suppose. Hey you said you had some long guns. What do you have?" Annie inquired.

"I got a 12 gauge, a .22 and a multi-rifle. Bet you never heard of one of those." Hogan said referring to the last one.

"A multi-rifle? What's that?" Annie said perking up with interest.

"I got a TNW Aero survival rifle with a multi barrel package. The particular model can shoot 9mm, .45 and 40 cal. pretty much any common pistol caliber I can find." Hogan said proudly.

"That is a sweet rifle! What I mean is that is a seriously cool rifle and useful too with that ammo variability. Are you going to let me borrow your shotgun?" Annie asked.

"You can borrow the Aero rifle if need be. I prefer carrying the shotgun for now. I usually pack that rifle in my boat's bow bag. I really like that secured storage feature on my boat. It is big enough that I can pretty much pack a whole 72 hour bag plus camping equipment or whatever I want in it." Hogan said before telling her he would show her what all he kept in that bag later when they did a repack of both of their gear.

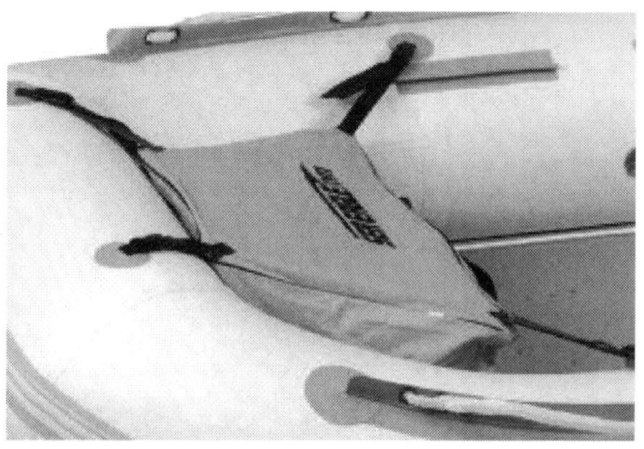

"I don't think I need to really repack anything; my bug out gear is pretty much ready to hit the trail on land or water now. I have lots of room in my Kayak for my gear and my food if I solo it." Annie said looking out the window.

"What's the longest that you have ever camped out, Annie?" Hogan said changing the subject and finally getting around to having that talk he wanted to with her.

"I guess about four days straight is the longest I ever camped out in the woods. I have thought about what a long term bug out would be like if that's what you're talking about. I can deal with sleeping out in the boonies a lot longer no problem. What is it that you're thinking about specifically?" Annie asked.

"Well I am not thinking bug out to the woods so much as taking a four or five week vacation on the river. Let's just think in those terms for now. What I am thinking here is that we hang around for a week or two and just play bug in quietly with the rest of the neighbors. If we don't see the roads opening up enough for us to travel south we will go on vacation for awhile downstream and avoid problems around here for awhile." Hogan offered.

"Going on vacation, Hogan? Really? You don't need to talk to me like a child, I understand the dangers the same as you. I hope you know that by now. Spit out whatever it is you got on your mind and be done with it!" Annie said quite angry at Hogan thinking he was talking down to her.

"Now don't be getting mad at me I wasn't putting you down in any way. I meant to call it vacation; you can call it survival camp if you want because I want to teach you a few things before we have to bug out for real one day. Have you given any thought about how long it's going to be before people get stupid desperate here? I don't mean just plain "I am hungry and haven't eaten in a couple days" desperate, I am talking will do and try most everything to eat as their mental processes go into delirium." Hogan said seeing her calm down immediately and furrowed her brow to ponder what he just said.

"I would say the first stages of hunger and desperation vary from house to house. I would say that you and me are prepared with enough food storage to sustain us for maybe two months, maybe much longer if you do any fishing or hunting. That is as long as we have the river to access for water. I am still worried about what pollution we might get but nothing we can do about that. However, most people in this neighborhood I bet are not even close to being as prepared as we are." Annie said still trying to estimate a meltdown point for the masses of people surrounding them.

"Annie, people will be eating whatever they have left in their cupboards and for a lot of people in this complex I am afraid that will not be much. You and I have a hard time understanding that some people can literally be out of food completely after only three days. I have seen it happen. One thing I discovered after talking to people about preparedness for a long time is that most of them live a pattern of eating out, picking up dinner on the way home from work, or buying just enough groceries for a few days." Hogan said letting her know things could get bad rather quickly for some.

"I was thinking about those kinds of folks and how they might be faring. I know quite a few people that are like that. Mostly younger folks do that but I know a lot of businessmen and women do it also." Annie declared thinking Hogan was the only person she knew outside her prepper friends at home whose lifestyle included having a bucket or two of rice and beans stashed away for a rainy day like this.

"I imagine the average person in this complex has only a week or so at best of food to rely on now and that won't be eating well either. Remember whatever frozen dinners and meats they got in the freezer will be bad in a few days. I don't think peoples exact situation has sunk in to them yet but it will. That's why I want us to take a vacation away from everyone for awhile." Hogan said letting the notion start to sink in.

"I get it! A vacation means we are coming back! Doesn't it, Hogan?" Annie said quite happy with herself for catching on so quickly.

"See I told you there was no reason for being mad with me. A vacation, let's take a nice long trip to the woods to meditate on nature and avoid some of the desperation and the crime in the city."

Hogan said making it sound more like a travel brochure than a short term bug out.

"So where are we going and when are we coming back? I probably know where we are going, your secret place on the river, right?" Annie said hitting the nail on the head.

"That's the place, as for when we are coming back, that depends. How does four weeks sound to you?" Hogan asked.

"That sounds doable. Why four weeks though out of curiosity." Annie asked curious how he had arrived at the timing.

"I don't know, it's pretty much just an arbitrary number I picked but I will tell you how I came up with that number later. If the road is passable and the cars still work tomorrow, then we will leave for Alabama. That is my preferred idea but I think it could possibly be impractical and maybe more dangerous than we realize. First thing to realize is that most likely we won't have radio for a few days at least so we will be blind about what is going on in the city or on the interstates for that matter. We would have to get out in traffic and go see conditions for ourselves and as you know a lot of these roads have places you can't get turned back around from once the road gets clogged. So that is maybe a bad idea. We don't need to go to the store so we stay off the roads also and avoid the bedlam. That's if the cars work mind you, if they don't, then we are really in serious trouble because that means we are stuck here." Hogan said as they discussed their plans.

"So when do we leave for our vacation then? I guess it won't really be a vacation though if we don't have working vehicles to come back to, will it, Hogan?" Annie asked wondering how this beast of a geomagnetic storm was going to affect them even further.

"If the cars don't work it won't be no vacation by a long shot. We will be stuck out on the river with no place to go and probably with a bunch of other hungry people getting hungrier in the same position. That is not the future I care to look at for us however at the moment. Say the cars do work, hopefully after four weeks or so the worst around here people wise will have gotten settled down some maybe and then we can try risking driving out." Hogan said opening their patio door they had closed for privacy but the temperature was getting stifling inside the apartment.

"It's not that much better temperature wise out here but at least there is a slight breeze." Annie said commenting on the heat as she walked out on the balcony with Hogan.

"I am thinking Annie that we need to siphon some gas out of the vehicles and lock it up in the apartment if we do decide to go on vacation. I am sure someone around here might need some gas and consider borrowing some from cars in the lot without asking if they are thinking about leaving town. We are going to need to do that siphoning thing at night or early morning if we end up doing that; I don't care to give anyone ideas, if you get my drift." Hogan explained.

"Are we just going to leave our vehicles parked right here? Not that I can think of a safer place to move them to though, mind you." Annie asked.

"I thought about moving them closer to where we are going to put the boats in at because it would be a safer spot if we were worried about fire but I decided against it. That place is away from any flammable buildings but you know whoever can, will be coming down there to fish. I thought about moving them over by the dumpsters too for fire safety but again all the foot traffic around here will be going that way for awhile to dispose of trash. That's another good reason to go on vacation; can you imagine what it's going to smell like around here in a couple weeks?" Hogan said thinking people would be throwing out a lot more crap than dirty diapers most likely.

"Leaving the vehicles sitting right out in front of the apartment makes sense then. It makes it look like we are home and maybe no one will bother them." Annie said considering that the gas in the tanks was less likely to be siphoned if someone was worried about getting caught in the act.

"Next question is how do we get the boats and all this gear and food down to the beach if the cars don't work?" Hogan asked regarding Annie with an "Oh NO!" look on his face.

"My Kayak is very easy to transport as you know inflated or deflated. I can wear my backpack and maybe load some food in my roll around suitcase and drag it along." Annie said before acknowledging that even with the wheels on Hogan's boat it was going to take several trips by foot to move boat, motors, extra gas, etc., etc. down to the landing.

"I could stay at the beach and guard stuff while you go back and forth bringing things." Annie offered.

"I see how you're going to treat an old man. I guess I am going to be the designated pack mule then." Hogan said jokingly scolding her.

"Well I can make a few trips for you and maybe you can rest and stand guard then?" Annie started to offer before she caught on to his small joke and smiled at him as he grinned devilishly back.

"We will work it out one way or another. Hey, do you feel like taking a walk with me down to the road? Not that there is anything much to see down there mind you. But that is the closest thing I can think of to my desire to get a news bulletin that I know of at the moment." Hogan said getting antsy about all this inactivity and lack of internet news to be speculating on.

"Sure I will go, did you notice that there are not a whole lot of cars that came back here after leaving earlier today? Well at least in our area, I don't know about the rest of the complex." Annie remarked.

"Yes I noticed, no telling where they are all at. They could be stuck in traffic on the far side of town or maybe they got lucky and made it out of the city if that is what they wanted." Hogan said.

"Well I for one hope they did make it out. I guess we will see what tomorrow brings and then we decide to stay or go." Annie replied.

"Annie, it's a cold world out there and we can't do anything to change it. All we can do is try hard to not let it change us personally and that will be impossible if we end up staying here for any length of time." Hogan said remorsefully.

"We will make it one way or another, Hogan." Annie said wondering about tomorrow.

I have learned that if one advances confidently in the direction of his dreams, and endeavors to live the life he has imagined, he will meet with a success unexpected in common hours."

-Henry David Thoreau

Sitting Tight

The eerie lights in the sky had quieted down and dissipated by around midnight. Annie and Hogan had said earlier in the day that they were going to alternate standing fire watch but the excitement of the previous day had taxed their bodies as well as their brains and getting some sleep seemed inevitable.

Hogan had asked one of the returning neighbors what they had seen out on the road when they drove in around 8 o'clock this evening and was told that the electrical substation about two miles up the road was destroyed and looked partially burned but no open fires were present. There were fires scattered around the city and the fire department and police were out in full force but they couldn't tell him much more because they had come in from the interstate loop and then the back way to get home. They didn't know what the conditions in the city proper might be. They said they had spent ten hours creeping along in traffic on a short stretch of highway just trying to get here and said the exchanges exiting the interstates were just as bad traffic wise. The good news was once you got a few miles away from an exit and into the neighborhood it was very light traffic with hardly anyone on the roads.

Hearing this news, Hogan had advised that he thought it would be alright for them to get some shuteye tonight but he voiced his concerns to Annie later about the apartment complexes smoke alarm system. Evidently it must have an emergency backup somewhere because the small red led light on theirs remained visibly on. Annie thought this evidently working alarm was a good thing at first and also expressed her surprise they hadn't noticed it previously. But of course everything was basked in the glowing reddish light of the storm so it was easy to miss.

Hogan said that although it was pretty cool that they might have some modern early warning of an impending fire to wake them, he didn't trust the system. He mentioned that if she remembered right the alarms had gone off during the storm and that their silence now while being operative might not be a good thing. Just because they didn't see any more Auroras didn't mean the geomagnetic storm was over or for that matter it didn't mean another one might not be on its way. They had already experienced two solar storms, why not three or more, he had asked?

Having evidently DC powered systems still operable was an exciting prospect but that also meant circuitry that could possibly catch fire later no matter how safe it normally was. Hogan reminded Annie what happens when you accidentally ground a car battery by crossing up the jumper cables or touching a car body with a wrench or a screwdriver when working on the positive connection of a battery. He also reminded her that most of these new lithium batteries people were using have electronic circuitry in them and don't have the built in fire retardant or anti grounding features his Relion Lithium battery did that he used for his trolling motor.

They both found it kind of odd and interesting that there would be a second lights out in the coming weeks then as battery operated emergency exit signs and lights would fail as the batteries run down. Technically speaking, the city would still have emergency lights on for awhile. Hogan jokingly remarked that particular fact would give everybody lights to loot by! He remembered how well lit up a Wal-Mart was in New Orleans during Hurricane Katrina and the media showing cops as well as regular citizens happily wandering around with shopping carts going down the aisles helping themselves to whatever they needed allegedly for free. It was blatant looting: grabbing shoes, electronics and many other non food or survival items but the mob mentality thought all this stealing was ok.

This free for all of looting spree didn't start up immediately in most areas and not until the media fueled the fires of peoples psyches with false as well as true reports about the hopelessness of help not being forth coming. Well this time the thievery might be different because the government had come right out and said nothing was coming for a month or so to a whole bunch of people that had been hoping and wishing for just this sort of thing to occur so they had an excuse to run amok.

On the flip side of that coin, Hogan also knew there were a whole lot of people that had plans to defend their stores and businesses from looting and surprises awaited the unwary in this no holds barred fight over goods.

Hogan and Annie had wisely decided they would stay in and avoid getting caught up in the crossfire of such looter business owner confrontations which was bound to be happening.

Some places would be better defended than others. For example, Hogan knew from a conversation he had with the neighborhood gun store owner previously. He and his employees as well as a few chosen friends had plans for defending that store's contents with overwhelming firepower until they could transfer the inventory to an unmentioned safe spot located in the country.

Big Hoss the proprietor of the establishment as the man was called, had jokingly or not advised Hogan that if he ever needed to find protection quick to haul ass in the direction of his store. This was because he and his crew would be loaded for bear as well as business. He planned on staying open and servicing his customers awhile if he could depending on the nature of a disaster.

Hogan had gone in long before this solar storm was predicted and just shot the breeze with the proprietor and his staff on several occasions. They had discussed about how stuff works in a disaster and Hogan was as interested in their plans as they were in his.

Everyone's expectations and actions are different in how they plan to overcome adversity or confront known threats. That's why the gun store had wire mesh on all the windows as well as a pull down steel door to secure it when they closed the business every night. Pretty much normal security precautions for a crime ridden city any gun store would have installed.

Hogan had seen and admired a lot of pictures on the walls of this gun emporium depicting their shooting team and hunting club and he had remarked that the man had his own standing militia if need be. The man then had given him a sly wink and reminded Hogan that he was a Class Three automatic weapons dealer also and showed him a picture and a YouTube video of him and his buddies shooting up one of the full auto gun ranges he owned out in the country not too far from here.

"Holy hell, you all look like Delta Force or something!" Hogan had joked thinking they looked pretty formidable just decked out and camo'd up for duck hunting in a photo but these suckers in a picture with UZI's and what not sitting next to their historic re-enactor authentic Gatling gun and civil war cannon was really mind blowing. They definitely had their destructive fire power bases covered.

Hogan had an open invitation extended to go shoot the cannon with them next time they took it out and he had really been looking forward to that. It was after the realization that that particular day would never happen when he and Annie started to speculate on whether or not that gun range might be one of the stores security rally points and maybe they themselves should be thinking about making their way there.

Annie thought that idea of the gun store employees being found there might be highly possible because no one in their right mind but a regular member of the range would think about approaching it in hard times. But neither he nor Annie had ever visited it before let alone become paying members of it. Hogan said that he bet ten to one Old Hoss was still hanging out at the main store and that they could maybe go visit with him and try to be a camp follower. That didn't sit well with Hogan though, too many unknowns to consider.

Annie wanted to consider it anyway and said they should lay all the pluses and minuses out like a continuity plan and evaluate what advantages they could gain by throwing their lot in with the evidently well equipped group. Hogan said they could; but it would just be a mental exercise because he had no intent on doing so.

"Why not, Hogan?" Annie had asked and was rewarded with a string of negatives starting with first "we don't really know them or what they stand for" and ending with "they probably wouldn't take us in anyway."

"Why not? We are prepared and have our own guns, ammo, food, boats, camping gear etc. what is there to object to?" Annie said trying to sway him to just go talk and hoping that if the owner was selling ammo they could get some more.

"Annie for ease of transport and room in the packs or on the boats we got plenty of ammo already. I don't see the risk in going there just for a couple extra boxes of ammo we don't need. That's why I got what I got in ammo already so I don't need to go out and take any risks or deal with unknown people." Hogan had fumed.

"Well you know some of these people on a friendly basis and they are about as likeminded as we will ever find I would think. Well I am not counting the cops that sometimes hang out there and might be in their hunting club or something but you said most of them seemed pretty much all right and didn't have that confrontational disposition when they were off duty. Don't they sell M.R.E's there also?" Annie said remembering some peanut butter packets Hogan had bought there and shared with her for their preps.

"They don't sell full meals there." Hogan reminded her because the owner evidently made bucks out of breaking down complete meals or buying overstock of basic components.

More food was going to be needed sooner than what Hogan thought no matter what form it took. Annie had argued and she had even threatened to go down there on her own but listened when Hogan had reasoned that they should between their two prepper heads be able to think of another alternative. They agreed rather quickly that rather facing the mob at the gun store even if they had somehow managed to stay open to do something else was sensible.

"Now what we want to think about going after maybe is what nobody else wants or has thought about yet." Hogan had advised to direct the conversation to more obscure alternatives.

"That's a hard one to think about! Everything that comes to mind people might not be actively seeking right now like bug repellant etc. maybe could be found on another aisle of another store we haven't thought of going to right now eh, Hogan? I have been trying to think of an alternate list of things like taking a trip to maybe a veterinary supply store for medicines, or possibly places people may not have thought of yet like food vending machines in an office building. Any place I can think of all carry there own risks." Annie had mused.

"As much as it sounds awful interesting and in some weird way exciting to join in the fray of maybe getting some free stuff for the taking now or later, it is still looting in every sense of the word at the moment. We aren't desperate enough to have to do it. It would be a very foolish thing to consider doing anyway. Every store owner is closing down their places and expecting trouble and every cop in the city is on duty." Hogan said wisely.

"Staying indoors and off the roads does sound like our best option. If we don't add anything to our food stores, how long do you think we can make it?" Annie asked.

"Well we don't have a lot for variety or thinking long-term subsistence but the food we do have on hand is so much more than most other people have to depend on for the future. We have got almost 100 lbs of rice and if we ate nothing but a pound of rice a day with some soy sauce on it between us; we have one meal a day for a 100 days. That's a hundred days longer than anyone who gets shot day one or lord forbid gets put in jail for looting right now. Day thirty and sixty we would still be sitting pretty with all those beans I got stored and that doesn't even take into account that month's plus worth of can goods we got between us. I tell you what, all those things that nobody wants right now that are not food products will still be behind the broken in store windows and such in a month or so and there will be a lot less competition for collecting them." Hogan advised having his feet firmly planted in his apartment at the moment.

"Like you said, no sense in us getting arrested or killed to just risk getting more of what we already got. Doesn't seem right however, for us to be just sitting around here and doing nothing though, do you have any other ideas?" Annie had asked before they concluded the conversation for the evening.

Hogan had awakened the next day with the same question running through his mind. If there was a power outage from a hurricane or something normally you just clean up your yard some and relearn the fine art of conversation again with whoever is around to talk to. You listen to the radio to hear how badly damaged other areas are and are thankful yours maybe has less trees down or something. You do this from morbid fascination and with nothing to do you might ride around to survey the damage in the neighborhood. After asking your neighbor if you happen see them in the yard picking up sticks and branches if they need anything, you also speculate with them on who has ice for sale in town and life goes on.

Then the days pass waiting for the power to come back on. The ice melts and the food in the freezer melts and gets cooked in the order it needs to sets the tone for the menu as it gets used up. You do this waiting and coping with the times game until the miraculous power of electricity restores your life and normal everyday living. Somehow you managed to gain a little bit more experience to do it all over again in a few years. Well they weren't waiting on power to be restored for life to resume as normal, so what was it they were they waiting on? This new life was going to be the new norm for a long time to come. One without electrical power and worse yet, no running water someday soon.

If he was back at home in Alabama, he had his gardens to get ready and wood to gather. Wood! They needed firewood! He and Annie could go see what sticks and twigs they could pick up around this manicured residential area before anyone else did and store it up for later use. That is exactly what task they could be doing instead of this nonsense about talking what to try to get a hold of that wasn't theirs this early in a disaster.

They brought their pitiful haul of make do firewood back to the apartment griping that the task heating up coffee water in the morning was going to be a foregone luxury all too soon. There was an extreme lack of burnable materials around here which would make cooking difficult after using up Hogan's propane and alcohol supplies.

They spent part of the evening talking about other places they could get to by car or boat to forage for wood and thought about the bands of people who would soon be forced to do the same.

It wouldn't take too long before every construction site and cabinet making shop was picked clean of combustible material they decided. That was something to put on their "to do" list they reasoned and then took stock of their fire fighting capabilities by wondering where some unattended fire extinguishers might be.

Chatter and speculations of foraging in the early days of an apocalypse carried on for a while with ideas and discarded suggestions. Hogan and Annie decided to deescalate their senses and go do some mundane chores to clear the mind before bedtime and packaged up some daily meals in smaller servings for awhile. Tiring of that chore and reasoning there was nothing left to do today, they retired to their respective sleeping areas...

"Hey, Annie! Good morning to ya! How long have you been up?" Hogan said wandering into the kitchen from his bedroom.

"Somewhere around dawn about an hour ago or so the sun light started coming in the patio door and freaked me out because I had a fire nightmare last night and I just stayed up off and on mostly." Annie said looking tired but cheery.

Hogan regarded her for a moment but was pleased she had taken the frightening awakening in stride. Not much more was said besides him saying that he was sorry to hear that she didn't sleep well and he had woke up once or twice to sounds in the night. Annie didn't comment any further so he went to the window to regard the new day starting.

"I made some coffee earlier, it might still be warm." Annie offered.

"Thanks! Did you come up with any missions for us to go on today?" Hogan asked as he went out on the balcony to check the percolator still sitting on his rocket stove.

"I thought that we could hook the battery cables back up on the cars and maybe make a little reconnoitering excursion around the area to check on road access and see what's going on with the businesses in the area." Annie said and explained she had already done the dishes and wished they had a bunch of paper plates stored.

"Is the water still on?" Hogan asked quizzically wondering if she had used any of the water they had stored to do the dishes.

"It's on and it is flowing better than it was trickling out of the tap yesterday but there isn't much pressure. Did you think of anything for us to do today?" Annie inquired.

"Yea I did, let's take my van and do your idea of riding the neighborhood but we will also gather as much wood as we can find before everyone else starts foraging for it." Hogan offered thinking that was one resource that would go quicker than anything else.

"We could go cut some green wood if you want; I noticed you had a saw in your gear when we were rearranging preps some." Annie offered.

"That's an idea, but we won't be around long enough for it to dry out much. Hey you know what I want to look at today... This might sound a bit crazy but let's go by the Post Office and see what's not happening there." Hogan suggested.

"Now that's an interesting concept. What's over there to look at beside a pile of undelivered bills and possibly interesting packages if one was to risk looking at them later?" Annie asked.

"I don't know, I do know that people sometimes use them for directions or as a place to meet up at when they are from out of town. It's a government building so maybe the National Guard might be around if they started mobilizing but I doubt it, most likely everyone is still trying to get to the armories if they decided to show up. Hell, a lot of soldiers just won't flat be able to get to their appointed drill areas because of the traffic jams. With all the communications down, it's going to be major confusion, pandemonium and probably even more grid lock on and around any of the major roads. I wonder what the cops and fire department are doing outside of having to send runners with messages to command stations. That's right, they can communicate with telephone hard lines between them and emergency management often times. That ought to be interesting; they aren't used to not being able to blabber on a radio when they need help or to direct an action. Radios ought to be up and functioning though soon enough and there are emergency cell phone towers they can bring in. Now on the other hand, maybe no radios because anything as big as those antennas they have to transmit and receive with at the stations that weren't disconnected they would maybe have fried." Hogan said wondering about the complexities of solar EMP.

While no one in the US saw it, felt it, or even read about it in the newspapers, Earth was almost knocked back to the Stone Age on July 23, 2012.

He had told Annie about that particular close call incident before and his suspicions about why it had taken scientists and the government to tell the public the entirety of it two years after the fact. They eventually advised us that the Sun had kicked out one of the largest solar flares and coronal mass ejections ever recorded during that period. They never did say why no one warned the populace back then that the solar storm had missed Earth by a whisker. If that thing had hit, we would still be picking up the pieces. That is, if we had somehow managed to pull it all back together after a catastrophic grid down situation we were totally unprepared for.

"Well I am about ready if you are, unless you're thinking about eating some breakfast." Annie said. She was ready right now to go do something, go do pretty much anything in order to get out of the apartment and see what was going on out in the rest of the world. A major societal shift had just happened, how were people responding? What sights were there to see?

"No thanks, I usually don't eat breakfast very often. There are some powdered instant breakfast drink pouches on top of the fridge if you want some. Or there are always the leftovers I think are alright from yesterday." Hogan offered.

"We ought to save all those concentrated calories in a package for our river vacation and put them in our bug out bags." Annie suggested.

Annie and Hogan knew that they had any number of new problems barreling their way now to contend with. They realized after a few more short days of them basically feasting on what was in the freezer; the grim game of day to day rationing of food survival would start in earnest.

"Good thinking, Annie! We will keep those foil packets put back as our emergency rations and not tap into them until we see the hardest days hit. The little bit of gas that we will use up in the car nosing about on a short trip to town doesn't worry me, but I just thought of somewhere that might be more interesting for us to go take a look at." Hogan said speculating on foraging as Annie waited for him to tell her where.

"I am wondering what the kayak livery on the river and the State Park look like." Hogan said with an eyebrow raised.

"I am curious about what is going on in those places also, but I am not so curious as to want for us to try to drive all the way over there to check them out. What's over there anyway that has you so interested to check them out?" Annie said regarding him.

"Well I am thinking it's more of an intelligence gathering mission I had in mind than anything else, except I do want some river maps if anyone is still hanging around the kayak place. I am pretty curious also what all those campers will be doing that might be still staying at the park campgrounds. They will run out of food faster than most I think is reasonable to say. I wonder if the Park Rangers are still hanging around or they have gone to check on their own homes first. Then there is the country club down that way to consider. I wanted to check in there out of curiosity also. There are a few other places to consider looking over and recon like where we put in our boats at usually. We won't most likely be using those boat ramps but others might. That will give us maybe some ideas and indications of what the river traffic is like." Hogan suggested.

"Maybe we will see the Yak Boys down that way. Depending on how far we go that's a fifty mile round trip. Can we waste that much gas?" Annie asked.

"We don't have to go all the way down that way if you don't want to; I was just kind of curious about the road conditions. Those roads are probably in pretty in much the same condition as they are around here anyway. But they would be interesting to see because we can get to some back roads that lead to the interstate that way." Hogan advised her while trying to figure out how best to escape this place. Working out how as well as when he would be able to gain access to a route remained problematic at best.

"I can see the point in us going to go undertake to drive over there then I guess. I know it's pretty early in the disaster, Hogan and most folks are behaving, but I can't help but worry about me having all that gear stored out there in my car. We can't afford to have any of it stolen now or later. Do you think that we should consider driving both of our vehicles down that way in case we can get a clear way out on the road and just keep on going?" Annie asked thinking they might as well try bugging out if they were already going down that way anyway.

"I thought about us doing that but I am still guessing that the highway is likely a huge mess with locked up exit problems going on at the moment. I worry about the traffic snarls less than I worry about the overzealous law enforcement types getting to break out all their zombie apocalypse gear and wanting to clear the exits any way they can and control those points. I don't like how police departments seem to like to be seen as a military occupying force versus a so called cop on the beat peace officer. We all know someone that gets way too exuberant and is the overreacting type of person that needs reining in to calm down about any adrenaline charged situation. That is why rookies in the police force get older stable hands to direct them and trainee soldiers get their over hormone selves directed towards doing more mundane tasks over and over that teaches them personal control and tones down the testosterone." Hogan said.

"Well I am sure they get plenty of practice clearing wrecks off the interstate anyway but I remember they had themselves some trouble getting protestors off the road awhile back." Annie said thinking if people were also trying to escape any fires or wrecks by foot at the moment.

"Both of those jobs I mentioned however take focused aggression that they are trying to build up in recruits to handle a situation. If someone has chosen a bad leader to put in charge, they can train people wrong or allow their charges to let out some of that aggression or judiciary force in the wrong direction. I am all for letting everybody blow off some steam if that's what they are going to do after getting themselves all hyped up on the theory the sky is falling and the lawless hordes are coming. Let everybody wear themselves out a bit more while some time passes if you want to call it that. Everyone right now is a shade too panicky to be around for my taste. Let me tell you something Annie, disasters are boring, dirty and heart rending, but mostly they can be boring. Ninety eight percent of the time this is the one time everyone in the community acts like they have a lot of good in them and since the cops are not messing with them for petty crap, everyone gets along. Cops then are actually respected and regarded for trying to help see everyone gets along in troubled times." Hogan said remembering how many times he himself had seen this community coming together of people during a disaster.

"I can remember a bunch of times I have seen on TV and the internet that law enforcement wasn't so nice during a disaster." Annie said thinking of a few instances like that mayor of New Orleans that didn't have the sense God gave a pump handle ordering gun confiscations on private citizens during Katrina.

"Oh I can tell you some idiocy abounds stories regarding government actions in disasters. An extreme example of testosterone fired idiocy is that cop that shot that retarded man 5 times in the back sniping from a bridge during Hurricane Katrina. You could say the media spin on making some of the most corrupt cops anywhere heroes in the headlines imagining that they were being shot at by lawless gangs (none of it happened, blatant lies just like the superdome horror stories, didn't happen, media spin) encouraged him to do what he did at his trial but I say not really. He had a bad moral character to begin with and a want to do it first. Also, he was known as an abusive cop they allowed to stay on the force. Those types of people don't last long though but they last long enough to cause a lot of damage, same as with a rogue soldier who is trigger happy shooting civilians in a war zone but that's quite a different story. Right now, I am thinking that we kind of play peon and say yes sir for awhile, if you know what I mean. Just like the village farmers do when the Federales and banditos visit and threaten the village in an old western movie. Or a better example is when Mr. Wong said he was fleeing to the mountains like they did in his home country when the communists took over. They go away for awhile, things calm down, and then they come back and start life again with less than they had before. That has been the role of countless poor refugees for centuries." Hogan said.

"But we are not refugees, we have prepared, we are PREPPERS! Hogan, you know as well as I do the whole reason behind the prepper movement is not to end up as a destitute refugee needing a spot and a cot in a FEMA camp. I can sort of see your point about letting people calm down some before us making a move but I thought the idea was to get out as quick as we can. People are already leaving the city in droves and we know the real lawlessness and chaos will soon come on its own around here." Annie objected and looked at him angrily that he seemed so indecisive when they should get out on the road.

"You haven't let me finish yet what I was trying to explain to you. It's the old theory of you go looking for trouble you will find trouble. Those poor peons and refugees I was talking about had no training in weapons or politics but they were good survivors, they can grow their own food, help their neighbors and get along, etc. They are always capable of moving on and starting someway again and plan for that. They prep for disasters also having experienced many in their lives already. They save food in good seasons to live easier after bad harvests, to flee from wars, to survive during long term sickness, etc. and they get by somehow. When a truly horrific country wide mass die off from starvation and war occurs like you see in old photos of Asia, humanity makes a move, the populace migrates. People begin to move as one big rolling mass and to save a sovereign country some food is provided by its overseers so that they and their base of power can exist. Call any of these refugee camps or FEMA camps that will spring up the analogy of that kind of governmental continuity if you want. When the US firebombed Tokyo during World War II or when we did the same to Dresden Germany and many other places, you had millions of displaced peoples on the move. Huge die offs occur on the road getting to a destination but many survive to carry on and teach another generation. The idea for an individual or a family is to not stick out like a nail that needs to be hammered during these times." Hogan said before Annie went back to her still wanting to get out before the upcoming waves of people that would be traveling hit the roads.

"We will get out of here, we could probably get out of the city right now I imagine if we managed to skirt around the outside of this city but what about the next one we come to? The roads of every major city and town will be a mess now. Who is to say it might not be worse in Columbus, Auburn or Montgomery? I have been stuck on roads evacuating from the Gulf Coast during a hurricane evacuation many times and they take a long time to clear out even a hundred miles inland. That is mostly going in one direction mind you away from a storm. Everyone everywhere wants to come and go to somewhere now in all directions. We don't know where it's passable on the road and where it isn't to get to anywhere yet. I thought you liked my going on vacation idea? See, depending on what it is we are going to be doing that time out or trip could wear many labels. We are going to be evacuating the city but not necessarily bugging out, if we leave our homes seeking refuge we are going to be called refugees and so on." Hogan said before jingling his keys at Annie that meant for her to 'come on lets go' in my van for a look see up the road.

"What is it that you envision we are going to be doing on this so called vacation of yours?" Annie asked as she looked out the vans window watching the very light traffic moving cautiously on the roads.

"Like I said, you can call it a survival retreat or hunting and fishing expedition or whatever else floats your boat. Mostly, we are just going to be out in nature and away from crowds and hungry people in general. The first thing I am going to teach you to do is how to snare a deer." Hogan said turning on the main road and then off again quickly pointing at what was possibly a wreck up ahead that would have stopped their forward progress.

"Well at least I see there are still some cops on duty. So you mentioned that deer snare thing before, do you have some pre-made modern animal snares for us to use or are you talking about teaching me to use some bush craft skills?" Annie said directing his attention towards a burned out building that was hard to tell if it was new or old damage.

"Annie, I am so glad this city didn't do a reenactment of the Atlanta burning thing from Sherman's March to the sea during the Civil War. There is plenty of smoke on the wind so we aren't out of the danger zone yet but I think mostly we have dodged the bullet for now. As for the deer snares, I will teach you both methods but I have a dozen hog size modern aircraft cable snares in my bug out gear. I have some of that 1500 pound test braided cargo cord also that is sort of like Paracord but is flat and soft to use for that purpose also. That stuff is made to support Army cargo parachutes; it won't break or twist up like a cable snare and is reusable. Now Annie I just had a great idea come to me from all that pressuring you been doing to get me to leave early. Calm yourself down now , I am just kidding with you, I have been ready to go myself ever since that emergency broadcast went off but I knew better than to try it." Hogan said grinning and hushing Annie to listen to his new idea.

"If we go on vacation, very early vacation that is, we will have the best success in our hunting and fishing efforts. You want to maybe start our vacation early like tomorrow maybe?" Hogan said thinking the wild game in the area wouldn't be under any pressure yet.

"Fantastic! Sure we can go, that's a good point about there not being a lot of hunters prowling in the woods yet. So is it that you are wanting to hunt and fish in order to save the canned goods or are we going to use them to supplement us if don't have any luck while we are gone?" Annie asked.

"Well we will be doing a bit of both I am thinking. If I can get a deer or two then we will be all set and I can cure some of the meat for food to take with us on our real bug out later." Hogan began.

"How are you going to cure it? You mean turn it into jerky? We already have been through that wasteful fiasco." Annie objected remembering the faulty stove drying out experiment.

"Hey that was a good idea if the power had stayed on long enough to get it all done. Anyway, I told you that we aren't done yet with that particular project. That meat will still keep with all that salt I poured over it and you had a bunch of it leftover to use for catfish bait like you wanted. If I had me a way to build me a smoker I could of maybe salvaged some of it that way, too. Or we could of solar oven'ed it and built one of those out of materials I have on hand. I forgot to tell you that I have five pounds of what I call 'pink magic' in that big plastic utility box in the van by the way." Hogan said running down his list of talents and ideas regarding the meaty mess they had both created that he didn't really care much about anymore. He still had his eye on eating up what frozen seafood they had left and unstable badly cooked meat that was probably just going to get thrown out and used for fish bait anyway, wasn't a concern.

"Is that pink stuff some kind of sugar ham cure?" Annie asked.

"No, but if I ever get the chance I might try that, probably make venison taste a lot better I am thinking. No Annie, what I have in that box is much simpler and cheaper than that sugar ham cure I am thinking you are referring to. You see before we had refrigeration available, curing was just about the only way to save up meat in warm weather months. Without salt, bacteria would grow in and on the meat and quickly cause it to go bad. The basic role of salt in curing is to dehydrate the meat just enough so that bacteria cannot thrive." Hogan said.

"So what kind of pink salt are you talking about? Is it like that pink Himalayan salt crystal lamp I have?" Annie asked thinking he was referring to a basket of food grade crystals on her dresser that gave off a nice warm glow when lit and were beneficial for indoor air quality due to releasing negative ions.

"No, that's not what I was talking about but thanks for reminding me that you have one of those, we have uses for that lamp later on seasoning or preserving food that we haven't considered. Hey Annie I have one those kinds of lamps back home in Alabama. The one I have though looks like a whole rock sphere carved out of one crystal. I got it for a gift from my lady one Xmas. They do make a difference in freshening up the air in a house." Hogan said remembering the planter shape holder of the warm reddish globe he had stared at many times before turning it off to go to sleep because it was deceptively bright in a darkened room.

"Well, that's about the only thing I can think of that resembled what I thought you were talking about." Annie said waiting for him to explain further.

"The one thing I think we should consider as the most important ingredient in my opinion to include when preserving meats by curing is sodium nitrate. Sodium nitrate by the way can be found in all kinds of leafy green vegetables and can be added to your salt mixture in the form of celery juice, ground spinach or pink salt. What I mean by that, is a kind of pink curing salt labeled #1, which contains a 7 percent sodium nitrate. Sodium nitrate is useful for warding off the development of one of the worst kinds of bacteria found in food — botulism. Sodium nitrate will also make your cured meats turn a nice shade of bright reddish-pink. That is more appetizing to the eye which means a better taste to the tongue and looks fresher if you know what I mean. One thing to be mindful of, however, is that high levels of nitrates (like most anything) are toxic and you need to be careful about the amount that you are adding to your curing mixture. That special curing salt I have is a commercial preparation and has the directions and proper measurements on the label, so no worries.

The stuff is reasonable and all the salt companies like Morton's etc. produce it." Hogan explained.

"Well that certainly sounds like we will get some good results by using it; I wish I had thought to have prepped some. So Hogan, are you pretty much proposing that we campout and practice our skills until it's time to leave from here and go to your house then?" Annie asked wondering what it was they were going to be doing while mankind was supposedly going to be going through some of its craziest times ahead.

"Yea, that's the general idea; we just hang loose and lay low. If we get ourselves located downriver and setup camp and start hunting early, we will have a chance to build up our supplies and avoid the BS around the apartment complex. Real soon I think things will start to unravel around here and if we ain't here we don't have to get involved in none of it. I ain't in the mood to watch the neighbors getting into squabbles or keeping an eye on my stuff every minute to keep it from getting stolen. If we just drop everything and go on vacation now we won't be committed entirely to any one particular course of action about bugging out and we will try to use the time to build up our reserves. If we can do all that while avoiding people and possible trouble in general by being somewhere else, let's go ahead and get on our way." Hogan said trying to get a glimpse of the river from a different perspective between two brick buildings as they passed.

"This is so weird for us to be able to see all these houses and cars and such sitting idle and think no more electricity and no more gas for either, ever again. I know that is probably a true statement but that fact just doesn't register in my mind yet. People still have gas in their cars, some houses have generators, most everybody has a flashlight and maybe some fresh batteries, but how long does all that last? I mean everyone is surely not just sitting around twiddling their thumbs waiting to run out of food and fuel permanently! They have to be working on something to help them survive! What are they doing? How are they trying to prepare? Mostly what I am thinking most about right now is where are all the people that normally live around here, at? I haven't seen hardly anyone." Annie said trying to make sense out of it all and wondering why the neighborhoods looked kind of deserted of anyone being outside digging a garden or doing whatever.

"I don't know what they might be doing but I know what we are going to be doing. Let's me and you leave for vacation as soon as the fridge gets empty back at the apartment maybe. Just go ahead and get us and the boats out on the river after we use up the food or do we take it with us. What do you say?" Hogan asked.

"I am all for taking some with us but let's see what we have left perishable wise when we get back!" Annie said excitedly thinking it sounded like a wonderful idea.

"Ok, so that's what we will do then. Just disappear ourselves for awhile and wait. We can use the time to plan the rest of our trip or talk about what we will do if we have to stay for some reason out on the river longer than expected." Hogan said relieved the tedium of watching the disaster unfold from the apartment was going to get some relief soon.

"So does that mean we will be taking anymore vacations later on?" Annie said quite happy that they were going to make a move soon.

"Could be, no telling what kind of road side attractions we might find." Hogan said kidding with her.

"Seriously though, Hogan, what's the long term plan? We haven't talked about what we are going to do if we have any problems down at your place in Alabama. We don't know conditions down that way. Also that would be getting pretty close to the end of the road for us gas wise since we don't know for sure where to get anymore at." Annie asked.

"I have been half considering that, it is pretty hard for me to speculate on even getting home let alone be thinking of having to do a secondary bug out. Hopefully most of the stuff that I got stored down there is going to be unmolested by the neighbors, but I wouldn't count on that being so for very long. That fact is quite worrisome to me but it can't be helped if I can't get out of here and reclaim my house in a timely fashion. We also don't know what road conditions are like down that way. I have already pretty much decided the best way to go back maybe is a little round about but we will parallel water most of the way following the Georgia-Alabama border on highway 27 south. If we get in trouble and the roads are not clear we can get always get back out on the water somewhere or find us an alternate route by car. Depending on road conditions I think we can swing off that highway for the Florida coast or head on towards my house. It only takes us a little out of the way to do either final destination." Hogan said dreading the indecision but thinking he had about as solid of a plan as he could make right now.

Northwest Florida and Apalachicola Bay was the only "Bug Out" locations he could come up with other than bugging in at his home at the moment.

If they could get to the town of Chattahoochee, Florida, they could continue the trip by water or by highway.

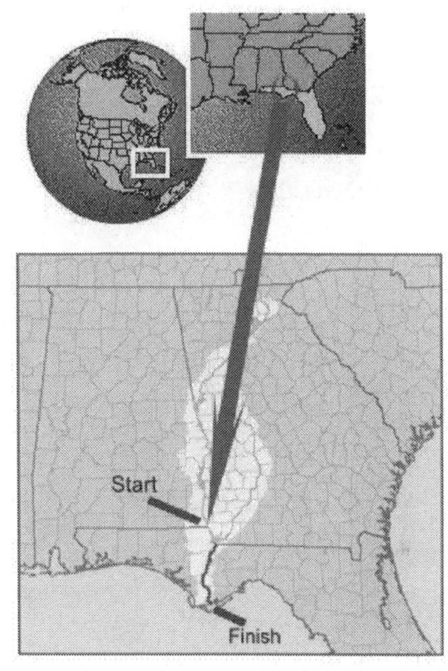

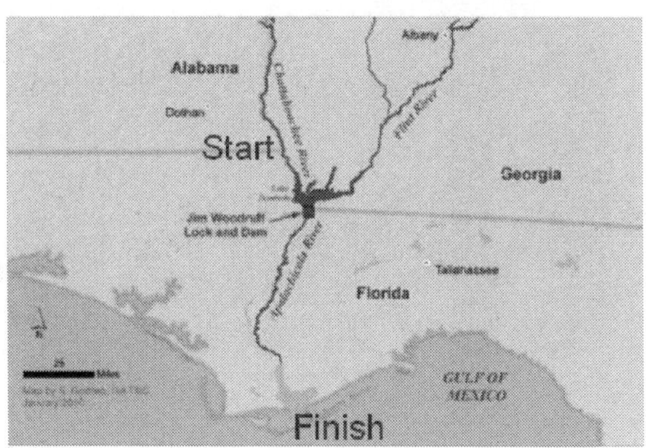

In the meantime, he and Annie discussed that the National Park Service currently maintains 12 boat ramps along the water trail they could use for their vacation. Six more are maintained by the cities of Duluth, Roswell, and Sandy Springs; U.S. Army Corps of Engineers; and Georgia Department of Natural Resources.

They were discussing which of these boat ramps they wanted to visit when they spotted flames off the road to their left. Apparently, an electrical substation was flaming out and the fire department was watching it but just letting it burn.

"Annie, you might want to tell those former neighbors of yours to please consider going inside and closing all windows and doors if the sky gets any blacker. That smoke is not safe to breathe! They might want to consider covering any cracks around doors and windows with tape or damp towels, if it gets real bad." Hogan said.

"I don't know what that is burning up ahead but I suggest you get turned around and head us back, Hogan." Annie said seeing traffic starting to slow.

"I agree, I will turn in that parking lot ahead and head back to the apartment." Hogan said turning on his blinker.

.

5

Smoke On The Horizon

Hogan and Annie spent the next few days eating up most of what they had left in the fridge and freezer and getting ready to go on vacation. They had been observing the comings and goings at their launch point the last few days debating on what the best time of day would be to put in their boats. There were very few fishermen surprisingly in this river side apartment complex. Well at least ones that had their rods and reels at home with them anyway and made the effort to go down to the little beach. Hogan had talked to an old man and his wife who were out there fishing early yesterday morning and asked about their luck catching anything, amongst other things. They said they had some small success fishing for catfish with canned corn and that using flour dough bait worked on perch and bluegills and worked pretty well in the early morning hours.

Hogan suggested that they consider to try soaking some of that corn in garlic powder as a possible fish attractant and he and the old man chatted as Annie talked to his wife. They were retirees and had moved here to be closer to their grandkids but their son had moved to another state up north for a job and they just sort of stayed here not wanting anything to do with snow at their age. The old man said he had given some hooks and line to one or two people who had asked him to sell them some, but he was kind of miffed they hadn't seen them since. The hulkster boys lived across the street from their building, the old man said and Nimrod (That was the biggest ones' name that Hogan found amusing for some reason) had offered to buy any excess fish they might catch from them.

Dixon (that was the old man's given name) looked away as Annie and his wife Marylyn started hysterically laughing at something and Hogan waited for Annie to clue him in on what was so funny.

"I have a feeling that I am going to be the brunt of that joke." Dixon said dryly before pausing.

"Old woman are you talking about me?" Dixon asked pretending to be angry.

"You know I am, old man!" Marylyn said with a much younger woman's giggle.

"I can't seem to get no respect." Dixon said shaking his head sadly and then gave his wife of fifty years a playful look with gritted teeth.

"Oh Hogan, you have got to hear this story!" Annie said laughing with her eyes all a twinkle.

"Let me tell him my side of the story first Marylyn before you start up with your teasing at me. I don't want Hogan and Annie thinking I actually am the daft old fool that you are about to make me out to be." Dixon said with a smile before starting to tell his end of an experience that had occurred the day before.

Dixon said he had been sitting with Marylyn talking about going fishing that evening for something to do more than needing food and was griping that they couldn't buy any crickets, worms or shiner minnows to do it with because the bait store was closed, they figured.

"We went by there; we are going back today to see if they open up. Dixon says that we can raise us some worms in a cooler on the back porch if we can get some." Marylyn said before apologizing and saying that she would hush and let Dixon finish his story.

"Well, as I was saying, I got to thinking about where to get us some bait and thought about the field in front of the apartment and all the weeds around the edges." Dixon said before telling the women to be still because they had started giggling again. After receiving the ladies smiling solemn promises to try to hush, he resumed his story.

"Well when I was a boy a century ago I thought nothing about catching bugs and such and figured what the hell I would go out and try my hand at it again. Let me tell you, Hogan, that isn't an endeavor you want to try at 76 years old, you kind of lose all your creepy crawly grabbing skills if you know what I mean. Either that or the grasshoppers have gotten a lot faster since I was a young man." Dixon said with a twinkle in his eye letting Hogan paint his own mental picture of an old man trying to catch bugs in a field.

"Marylyn, you are busting to tell this story so go right ahead." Dixon said with a smile watching his wife who was on pins and needles with Annie to get the story out to Hogan.

Marylyn forgot all about her fishing line in the water and laid her fishing pole down on the bank and her and Annie came over and sat next to the two men.

"Well I had come out on the back patio to sit and wait for Dixon to come back. You can't see much of the field from our porch but I felt better being out there where I might hear him or something, if he needed me. Well you know how they have those concrete wall dividers between people's patios? The neighbors come out and didn't know I was sitting outside next door and they commenced to getting their grill going and evidently their little boy saw Dixon attempting to catch something." Marylyn said before Dixon interjected his opinion on that family.

"When they ain't listening we call them people next-door the neurotic ones. They are scared of their own shadows." Dixon said hotly before Marylyn paused her story long enough to tell Hogan they had got branded with that moniker when she and her husband had observed awhile back their little boy get his first tricycle. She explained he wasn't allowed to use it unless he had on his helmet and knee and elbow pads and such.

"Why I have seen dirt track motocross racers wear less safety equipment than they force on that little nipper. I bet that skinny snowflake won't ever get the chance to experience a real boy's fun of growing up and discovering things in nature. Hogan, I heard a screech one day and a commotion going on next door to us and peeked around the corner through the privacy fence and saw her clutching that little goomer in her arms in the corner like an attack dog or something was after them. The husband, he come out and bravely stood in front of them with a silver spatula, a kitchen tool mind you, extended out in front of him bellowing for something to get away and backing up and smushing everybody more into the corner of that tiny patio. I thought it was a poisonous snake or something so I hollered for them to hold on and I would come to help and asked was their gate open? I grabbed my shovel and stood on my bench to see over the top of the fence to figure out what it was that had them so upset and do you know what it was? A lizard! Nothing but a big old danged green lizard that was puffing up his red throat trying to look cool for the lady lizards! That trivial thing is what they were scared of so bad" Dixon said chuckling.

"They got under my skin when Mrs. Blatt, how's that for a last name, decided after she was watching Dr. Oz or something on the TV that I had to give her a list of all my flowers that I had growing out on my deck. Now she had something with that notion or worry I have to give her credit for. I didn't know about poisonous flowers being so common. Did you know Begonias contain poisons called insoluble oxalates that can kill dogs and cats? They say if your pet manifests symptoms of begonia poisoning they will start drooling, vomiting, have problems swallowing, exhibit burning and visible irritation of the mouth, lips and tongue. I had no problems removing mine but they don't even have a pet! They were scared little Lord Fauntleroy would get his hands through our fence and poison himself. They made the apartment manager put a list of banned plants in the complexes rules and wanted the maintenance guys to inspect the property for suspect plants. Ha! I bet them idiots couldn't tell you a daffodil from a daisy." Marylyn concluded.

"Get back to the story!" Annie encouraged.

"Oh yea, so I am listening to those nitwits next-door and they are speculating on whether or not Dixon here has lost something in the grass or if he has gone senile while doing whatever it is he is doing because all they see is him busy stumbling around sweating and cussing. Now I think what I am overhearing is funnier than hell and was biting my tongue to keep from laughing out loud but decided I needed to go retrieve Dixon because they started saying they thought he might be having an onslaught of an epileptic fit or dementia. Now since I can't see him I get worried and start wondering if he hasn't gotten himself a case of sunstroke going on maybe from chasing around out there and go to see about him. Well, that's when the fun really started! You see the Mr. Blatt's mom and dad live in this complex also and they were walking their way over here for a visit. Evidently, Dixon had given up by now his idea of pursuing fish bait out in that hot field and was heading back to the apartment." Marylyn said reaching over to hold her old hubby's hand.

"Now she is going to accuse me of being a dirty old man! But I am not, I swear!" Dixon said objecting and after a light squeeze on his hand he let Marylyn finish the story.

"Well to hear him tell it what happened next was he saw a Monarch butterfly and tried to give his ancient insect catching capabilities one more go so he started chasing after it."

"Darn near got it too!" Dixon exclaimed before hushing so that Marilyn could carry on with the story.

"Well that butterfly flew up on the wall and landed. The way he tells it, that butterfly landed about four feet off the ground on the corner molding of the building. Dixon said he tried sneaking up on it with his hands cupped together to catch it and missed it. The butterfly then began to fly around the corner of the apartment building with Dixon in hot pursuit with his hands outstretched in front of him and he grabbed at the first black and orange thing that he saw. What he grabbed wasn't what he thought it was though. Turns out old Mrs. Blatt and her husband chose just that same moment in time to be walking their old selves between buildings and she had on an orange and black print blouse that Dixon's fingers tried to take a liking to." Marylyn said busting out laughing.

"Course I had my momentum going and got my feet all tangled up in the excitement of the moment trying to dive around that corner to catch that butterfly. I swear Hogan, I didn't know what I had a hold of at that time but it ended up being Mrs. Blatt's over large flouncy blouse collar. You know one of those big ruffley bib looking things that sort of look like butterfly wings and are made out of some kind of light and airy fabric? Well I let go of what I was trying to cup both my hands around and we sort of fell into Mr. Blatt and we all ended up falling on the ground with me on top." Dixon said as the skin around his eyes wrinkled with mirth and he could hardly contain himself from outright busting out laughing at the spectacle.

"That is when I came around the corner from the front of the building and saw that dog pile of people. Reminded me of playing football as a kid! Would have been funny if I wasn't so concerned about a bunch of old people wiggling around and looking like they were turtles turned over on their backs!" Marilyn said with a loud guffaw and drank some of what appeared to be red Kool-Aid she had put in a normal spring water bottle.

"You see I had gone out the front door of our apartment so the neighbors didn't know I had been listening to them to go check on Dixon. We sort of avoid talking to the neighbors if we can if you know what I mean because they are so problematic you might say. Anyway, the neurotic neighbors are rushing out the wooden back gate of their patio to find out what just happened as Dixon is trying to pull up Miss Blatt from off the ground with her dress riding up and the husband is hollering 'don't touch her pervert'!" Marylyn said barely able to get it all out before she started laughing again.

"This is the part I like!" Annie said joining in the merriment.

"That guy had that same damn barbecue spatula in his hand that he tried to fight the lizard with!" Dixon said slapping his leg in glee after holding up one finger to set up the next revelation of that funny event.

"Well here I was trying to help that old biddy up and her husband I guess thought I was trying to molest her and here comes this son of theirs to splat me with a burger flipper." Dixon said taking a sip out of his wife's water bottle.

"So what's a man going to do I says to myself in this situation and let go of Miss Blatt, who landed back on Mr. Blatt and tried to fend off his son who was trying to fly flap me with a spatula! Now I don't know about you, but I take that kind of threat seriously even if he hasn't tried to use the edge of it on me and I try to kick him in the knee. " Dixon said before his wife cut him off and advised "and he fell on his butt again!" to which they evidenced disagreement with the account of that particular operation regarding its alleged defensive moves outcome that was solved with a couple glances at each other before carrying on.

"I hollered at him to put the spatula down and Dixon started trying to get his feet under him when that squirrelly man tried to hit him as he was getting up. So I clocked him!" Marylyn said.

"She did more than that! She knocked the danged doo doo out of that boy. Got him square on the chin and kicked him in the butt on the way down!" Dixon said clapping his hands together laughing before reaching over to give his wife a kiss.

"I just reacted; someone was trying to hurt you." Marylyn began before saying "I knocked the crap out of him, didn't I?" before wincing and saying her hand hurt.

"That you did darling, you would of probably tussled with his wife too, if I would of let you." Dixon joked.

"Anyway, I got back to my feet Hogan and picked up that old spatula he dropped and told them all that this wasn't anything but a mistake and a big misunderstanding and to calm down and behave. I also told them a time or two that I would whoop their asses with it like very bad children, if they didn't behave and EVER tried fighting with me and my wife again. Sorry, Hogan and Miss Annie, but them marshmallow millenniums are out of their element thinking they can take on a pair of old style Arkansas razorbacks like me and Marylyn. Once things settled down and the stupidity of it all got understood, we had us a nervous laugh and left. More of an understanding that everyone needed to go home, if you get my drift. That guy was actually going to crown me and his dad was holding me until good old momma here threw a haymaker at him." Dixon said.

"Yea it wasn't no Mayberry comedy fight, we were seriously trying to hurt one another but it was still funny. I bet them people never been in a fight in their lives let alone lived through some of the bar brawls that me and Dixon have seen." Marylyn said.

"I can imagine, I am glad you didn't whoop up on them much even though you could have. Still funny as hell though, I agree. So give me more details about that little fracas." Hogan said smiling.

"He wasn't hurt much, cut his lip was all and got surprised as hell but I don't reckon she loosened any of his teeth." Dixon said breaking into his backwoods interpretation of a hillbilly drawl that is often imitated in the neck of the woods they came from.

"You have got to find some younger folks to chase bait for you while you fish." Annie suggested grinning.

"I was just telling Marylyn that very same thing. How screwed up these days is it that you can't get an over active seven or eight year old or whatever that whiny butt kid is, to catch an old man and woman a bug to fish with? I know they don't fish, I know they can't clean one or have the intestinal fortitude to bait the hook maybe. Marylyn, do you think them neighbors are vegetarians? Those were soybean burgers they said they were cooking on the grill last time we asked." Dixon fumed.

"No but it seems like I smelled them cooking meat over there before ... I never really gave it much thought. Those folks worry the hell out of me now because they are so pitiful in just facing life on an everyday basis, well life as I know or remember it anyway. So the kid gets banged up a bit playing with his tricycle, we all did. We also had our parents around to catch us and avoid those falls they had to experience themselves to avoid and look out for us so we didn't get any boo-boo's. Reminds me of those Yankees that put their little kids in them star shaped snow suits with so many layers of clothes they can't move." Marylyn said remembering when she was a little kid they could run around half naked and survive just fine in the bright sunshine and rusty red clay dirt of the back roads of her minds upbringing.

Hogan broached the subject with them about how they planned on getting by in this little apocalypse that everyone was just starting and asked did they have any sage advice for him and Annie.

"Oh, we are full of advice but none that you probably would do after you listened, this is a young and old persons world of doing exactly what we want to and ignoring others and elders it seems. I could tell you my firsthand experience of growing up during the depression and what our parents did while waiting on electricity and indoor plumbing to come to town. What they did with their lives and what went on in ours is all forgotten eras compared with the present experiences we are living now, though. Each of us look at the current situation with different eyes. Me and Marylyn are going to die Hogan; we haven't given up, don't get me wrong, we are simply going to expire before our time you might say and we accept that. No regrets because age is a drama only the experienced care to keep living. We have 30 days each of more pills than we can keep up with that the doctors have prescribed to make us supposedly live longer. Which pills those exactly are we have forgotten because the other pills are to offset the side effects for the ones that make us live longer. Never take pills, Hogan. I would tell you that bit of advice and you will probably live better and better. Anyway the pills will be gone and the diet restraints are already out the window and me and Marylyn here are going to sit and fish until our times come around.' How about you two? Got anywhere to go, anything to do?" Dixon asked as the shock came to Hogan that neither he nor Annie had considered that basically what they would call everyday functioning elderly people these days would go downhill quickly as soon as the medicines run out. Both of them were familiar with the regime of medicines that were often given previously to older parents. Hogan and Annie didn't take any daily doses of medicines themselves but that was not the norm it seemed with the general populace with drugstores opening on every corner. You had to ask why they existed and more were built when not long ago a few used to serve very large cities.

It is like folks were being destined to time warp and start dying or something as soon as you were issued a script from a doctor because many modern prescriptions were so powerful you needed another doctor's supervision to get off of them.

"Don't look so sad you two, we have lived ourselves a full life and might just beat the banshee on this one. What I am saying, is that we are at peace with the dying sooner than later, that is if the neighbors don't give us a heart attack first." Marylyn said chuckling.

"You need to teach someone everything you know about surviving before you two decide to check out. Why I bet you got a million stories you will need to get out in the coming days that might just keep you ornery enough to just keep hanging around to aggravate folks a bit longer!" Hogan said trying to lighten the subject and encourage this engaging couple to hang on.

"Like I said, I am pretty sure that I am going to be here with my wife a lot longer than most of these young folks that don't have a clue what to do now. We know how to get by in hard times, don't we, sweetie!" Dixon said playfully towards his wife who gave him a quick affirmation.

"That's why I gave those young ones some hooks and line when they said they wanted to buy some from me. I just upped and said here take it. What are we going to do with money? Nothing, especially when you know your days might be numbered. I wanted to give them a chance for them to live a bit longer I guess and I wanted to feel good about myself about doing it. I could tell that they didn't know much about fishing except maybe there daddies taking them out a time or two when they were growing up. I could have taught them something and maybe they could of helped me and Marylyn some. But you see that is not how they think these days. They have maybe looked at something on the internet like fishing and figured it was an easy task with no experience to do, but we both know the fallacy in that, Hogan. You see, the art of training dogs or young ones is lost if the adults were raised wrong, we been raising generations of wrong for years and you can't just give people or animals what they want when they want it." Dixon said.

"People need a straight path to stay on that has consequences if you veer off of it to keep you guided, you might say. I have watched the two of you all by the way, that's what old people do we are nosy and watch people. You look out for each other's safety when you are launching your boats or fishing from the bank because you are used to standing next to each other and working together to get something done. Young people these days just like we did, think they are smarter than a different generation. I think it is different now though for this one because the access to answers from the internet makes it difficult for them to judge others any different. They don't go ask old or more experienced people for answers and they don't interact much with others except through social media. They stay in their own sphere and if they are not too crazy about whom it is delivering the message or their own introverted ideals of who can give such information, they don't listen." Marylyn said voicing her opinion.

"Well, not to cut you short Dixon and Marylyn but we were just wandering by for a short visit However, you sparked an idea in me that I absolutely have got to get out and get your advice on. Times being what they are we are kind of pressed for time, if you know what I mean. I want to give you something for one thing and by doing it I hope you know I consider it bestowing a treasure upon a treasure. Annie, would you mind grabbing the extra trot line and GULP bait I showed you the other day and bringing it back here?" Hogan asked.

"I will come with you honey to get it." Marylyn said used to such spontaneous outbursts that tended to indicate the men folk wanted to talk in their redneck way as the womenfolk used their intuition to guess what it was and do some of their own.

"I am going to give you that trotline and a few things, Dixon." Hogan said.

"What am I going to do with a trot line Hogan, when I can't get it far enough out in the river to take advantage of its length?" Dixon said bewildered.

"You don't have to rig that trot line a particular way and I am sure when you think about it you will come up with some unique solutions of your own. What if you could leave a legacy? I don't know the specifics of your ailments but you need help right now and some additional help sooner than later. I think I might just have a way to help you out, so listen up, please. As far as we know at the moment, we will call you the top dog fisherman around here. That gigantic weight lifter that is your neighbor and his friends need food and they have already said that they are willing to pay for it so what you do is take that set of puppet strings I am about to give you and you and your wife play them boys like a cello to help yourselves out."

"Just what is it you're talking about old, son? Now I would be danged grateful for that preprocessed GULP fish bait and the floating trot line but I do not understand the rest of that talk you are doing. Well maybe I do, is what you are saying Hogan is for me to get these young folks around here involved in fishing and maybe they could help me some for providing the tackle and the knowledge to get it done?" Dixon said studying him.

"Yea they can help catch bait for that trotline rig, feed themselves and if you get can get them to do a little security work to keep you from molesting old ladies or whatever, so much the better. You should organize with them a community fishing effort maybe, there are 120 hooks on that trot line. You won't have that kind of luck but you should be able to pull a few stringers full of fish off pretty regular. Maybe you all can possibly figure out how to use that fancy grill of theirs to smoke some fish if it works out." Hogan advised.

"Molest this, Hogan!" Dixon said flipping Hogan the bird before carrying on.

"Could be, I wish one of them had a boat though. Guess somebody is going to end up going swimming to get that fish getter set up right. They are all young and athletic, that shouldn't be a problem. You know, Hogan, when I was a boy me and a bunch of friends went down the river from Chattahoochee Florida to Apalachicola. It took us an entire week but we had a great time, remind me to show you some pictures of that trip sometime. I know this river in bits and pieces, I bet you never traveled its entire length have you, Hogan?" Dixon said.

Photo credit Kevin Dougherty.

"No, but I have considered trying to do it. Tell me if you would, can you put in before the town of Chattahoochee, can you get a clear shot all the way down river?" Hogan asked.

"Oh yea, I guess the easiest place to put in at would be Lake Seminole on the other side of the dam lock. Hey, Marylyn, you got a fish on!" Dixon said pointing at her bobber going under.

"Guess she wins the bet on whoever catches the first fish today. That means me as the loser will have to clean all the catch for the day. I want a retry, Marylyn. It wasn't a fair contest! Why, If I wasn't sitting here talking to our company Hogan and Annie, I might have even won the catching the biggest fish bet." Dixon said playfully bragging.

"No, I won the bet as is and fair and square, nobody told you to stop fishing! You forfeited is what you did!" Marylyn said with a grin having Dixon dead to rights on that technicality.

"I guess you got me there. She snuck one in on me, Hogan." Dixon said with a smile as he finally got around to baiting his hook and flinging it into the water.

"Yea, women can be down right tricky sometimes." Hogan said smiling back before then asking Annie to come with him to go back to the apartment and work on a project.

As they walked back to the apartment they could hear the old couple happily bantering back and forth about whether or not a rematch was in order and chuckled...

One Foot In The Water

"Morning Annie, are you ready for some coffee?" Hogan said cutting on his propane stove burner.

"Sure, are you going to be bringing that big stove with you when we go out on the river?" Annie asked looking at the big unit

"No, I am going to be leaving it here; I got plenty of stuff to keep up with already." Hogan said but in the back of his mind it said take it with them also.

"I was just thinking that since we are basically setting up a base camp for ourselves that it might be a good item for us to have around in case it rained or something. I was also wondering if you were thinking about leaving it here in the house or packing it in the van. Which do you think would be safer?" Annie asked wondering about the safety and security of all the gear they had left loaded in their vehicles that were staying behind.

"I guess the apartment might be more secure if you have anything in particular that you're leaving behind that needs guarding better. Most of my gear is coming with me so I haven't given it much thought until now." Hogan said looking over the apartment at what little bit of gear remained.

"I still have some room in my boat if you need it." Annie offered.

"Having our boats easily accessible during this catastrophic event is sure a positive game changer. I certainly got a bunch of stuff! We can pretty much carry everything that we got with us because of those inflatable boats huge load capacities, though. Now I am not one for carrying the kitchen sink with us even if we can. Lots of this stuff I am leaving in the apartment because we don't really need even if we are staying out in the woods for a long time. If I bring all this of this prep stuff it would mean I got to load the extra gear on and off the boat also which is a pain, as you know. Besides, I would rather have the appearance of a smaller less equipped prepper footprint for others to see if we meet someone camping, if you know what I mean." Hogan said.

"Do you think we will see many people, Hogan?" Annie asked.

"I am hoping that we won't be seen at all hiding up on the rocks but I can't guarantee that. The absence of river banks in that area for travelers to beach at make finding a place to stop at for the night increasingly difficult so chances are we won't." Hogan said and then voiced his worry that any paddlers or motor boaters would be scrutinizing the banks and most likely looking skyward at times for smoke.

Hogan could build a pretty smokeless campfire when he considered concealment but he needed to work on that boat bush door thing of his better to hide that little run off notch he was going to use to access his boat cave camp.

He had not explored the cliff face that formed the left wall of that entrance much. You could get up to the top of its craggy edifice easy enough but doing so took you a good distance away from the river.

He didn't want to be far from his boat so that meant he was sort of limited in his camping areas. That was unless he deflated the boats of course and they drug them back in the woods which wasn't one of the items on his to do list. No, they were just going to stay where they pulled in at and conceal the boats as best they could with a camouflage net he had. He had jokingly said that netting doubled as his duck blind when he showed it to Annie and he might yet try that idea out for real one day. He wasn't too worried about doing that though; he saw ducks out on the water all the time and didn't need to hide from them if he wanted a duck dinner.

One thing that Hogan worried about that rocky bluff that concerned him was that if anyone got up on it they could see right down into his camp. The trail going up the side of it was not something that he would want to try to attempt at night, either. This caution was because it could be treacherous if you weren't watching. Hogan had considered making his camp up on top of it when he had first found the rocky clearing but had dismissed the idea.

He hadn't wanted to carry his gear that far up from the river then, now his reason was more than the labor of the chore that made him hesitate. He remembered a wild brush fire he had seen in the news once of one sweeping a ridge similar to the one he had chosen to live next to. Getting cornered on a ledge by anything including fire wasn't going to happen to him, he decided.

Hogan said that the best place for him and Annie to be camping would be only a stones throw away from his boat. The lower elevation for now was safer especially if they found they suddenly had to leave at night.

"Ok, Annie I think it is time for us to get this show on the road." Hogan said rising and heading for his front door with a few backward glances.

They got in their cars and headed for the apartments little river bank and were rewarded with seeing that the bank was clear of people. Hogan opened his vans hatch and pulled out his boat while Annie unlocked her trunk and got out her Kayak. They spread out and unrolled their boats a distance apart because this took up quite a little bit of room in the parking lot. Then they busied themselves getting ready to launch with all that gear and grub.

"Want to use my electric pump, Annie?" Hogan offered.

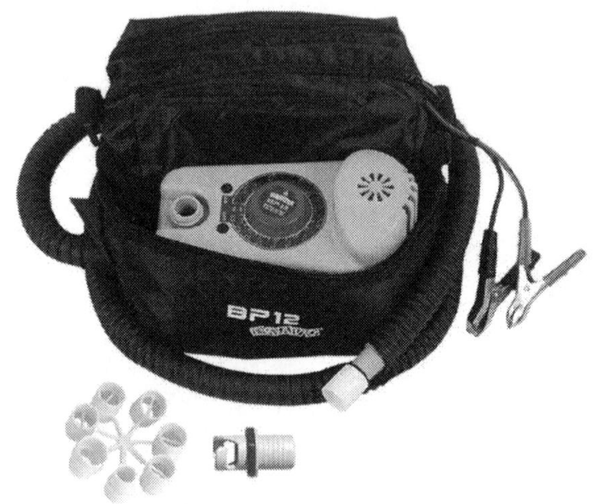

"No, I will probably have mine inflated and launched with my manual pump by the time you get that pretty Cadillac boat of yours put together!." Annie joked.

"Hey, perfection takes time! But I bet it won't take me more than about 15 minutes or so before I will be ready to put it in the water. Now, loading the boat after I launch it is going to be another story." Hogan said with a smile and he went back to his van to retrieve his aluminum seats and Bimini top canopy.

Annie had seen Hogan get ready to deploy his boat before and knew the best thing for her to do at the moment was stay out of the way. Hogan hooked the air pump to the first of five recessed one way valves he needed to attend to, hit the switch and then went back to the van to secure his Watersnake Venom 34 lb. thrust electric trolling motor.

He easily one handed its 15 lb weight and set it down on the pavement and then set the 12 volt battery down next to it.

"That always freaks me out that you can just wander away from that pump and it shuts off on its own." Annie said mentally picturing Hogan blowing up his boat but knowing it wouldn't explode because the pump would shut down at the right air pressure.

"I love how that auto inflate works to fill my boat to whatever air pressure I set the pump at. You see how quick this pump is? That is one thing I am always amazed about! I could have easily filled your kayak and my boat with air several times with just the juice in that little battery in the carrying case." Hogan said already aware Annie knew he could also run the pump off alligator clips and his car or trolling motor battery. Just for fun, he had also showed her how he could use an inverter off either battery or use the charger that came with the pump kit and use a wall socket to recharge its pump motor battery.

"Yea, that electrical pump is pretty awesome but I know that you have two manual backup pumps that came with the boat also around here somewhere." Annie said smiling.

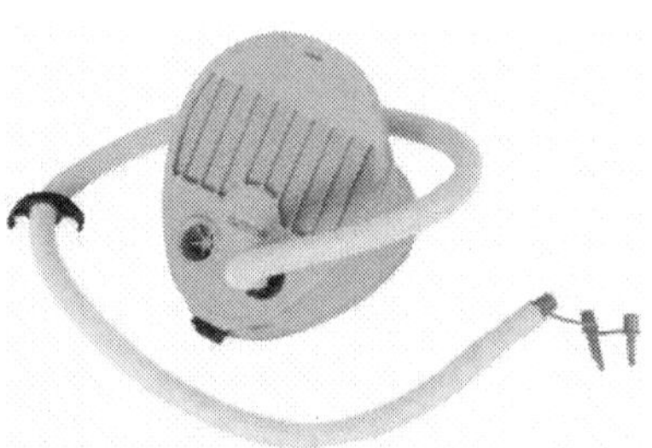

A41 Large Bellows Pump

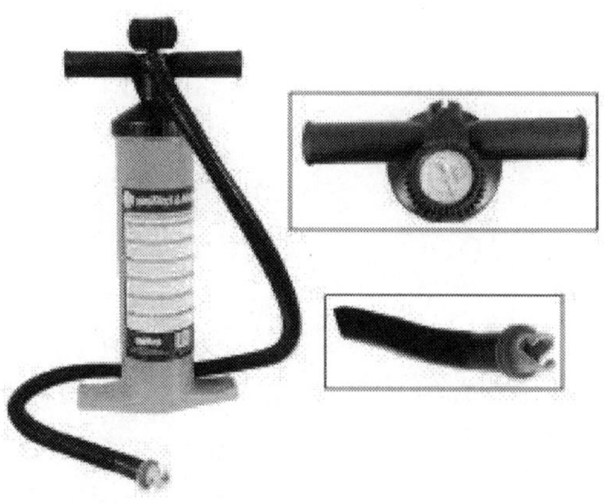

Dual Action Auto Two Stage SUP Pump w/ Pressure Gauge

"You know me; I have backups to my backups for some things. I bought me another patch kit also to have in my preps." Hogan said not wanting to leave anything to chance.

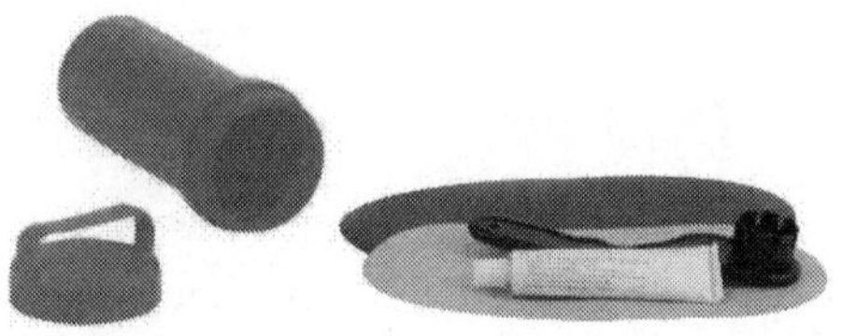

Repair kit for 1000 Denier PVC boats. Includes hull repair material, tube of glue & Halkey-Roberts valve replacement tool.

"Well, I certainly see the wisdom in that. Hey, here comes Dixon and Marylyn. "Annie said waving to them.

"Dang, I was hoping that they were staying in today." Hogan whispered and then smiled and waved at the old couple making their way towards them. Hogan didn't mind them seeing the boats but loading them to the gills with so much equipment for just going on an alleged camping trip would cause some questions and he was short on suitable explanations.

"Hey, good morning to you two! You all are kind of getting yourselves late starts on fishing today, aren't you?" Dixon said as he shook Hogan's hand and Marylyn gave Annie a hug.

"Well, we are not just going fishing, we are going camping also. I figured it was a good time for me to maybe hunt a deer before everyone started shooting up the woods." Hogan said busying himself while the boat was inflating by attaching the oar locks and paddles by thumb screwing them to the special hull mounts.

"I guess if you are thinking about going hunting, now is the time to do it. But I bet you ain't the only ones thinking of doing it." Marylyn said cautioning them to be careful.

"Oh I bet there is going to be folks out doing both fishing and hunting already, just not as many now trying their luck as later. Hopefully, they will have a clue what they are doing with firearms and practice some good gun safety." Hogan said thinking even a .22 caliber bullet could kill at a mile if someone missed their target.

"You might think about wearing some orange." Dixon said looking at Hogan's camo pants and OD vest. Annie had similar going to the woods garb on and was supposed to share the advice Dixon was giving indicated by his looking over at her.

"That's a thought, but I bet since everyone isn't worried about a game warden at the moment no one will. All the Rambo types won't be wearing any orange and probably are all putting on their camo face paint and thinking about breaking out a Ghillie suit or something." Hogan said now doing the last chore of fully inflating his boats drop stitch floor which only took a minute. When this highly engineered special floor was inflated it became rigid enough to stand on and to hold cargo. He really liked that feature and its nonslip texture. He had looked at some other manufacturer's inflatable boats that had solid wood or plastic floors and decided on the Sea Eagle for its weight and non slip air flow deck. The great advantage of the type of runabout was its light weight in relation to size because of the inflatable floors. That increases stow-ability and reduces the overall hull weight by nearly 30%. It also reduces the storage foot print by 50% because you no longer have to deal with wooden or aluminum floorboards.

"What is a Ghille suit?" Marylyn asked

The name Ghillie comes from Scotland where the ghillies were gamekeepers. Basically, it's a head to toe colored burlap suit that makes you look like a swamp monster or something. Military snipers use them a lot." Hogan said explaining.

"Wow that floor airs up solid, doesn't it?" Dixon said pushing against the floor of the boat with his hand.

"That 4" floor is one of these boats best features. It is made up of thousands of tiny threads that connect both the top and bottom layers, creating a stronger link that can withstand much higher pressures. Higher pressures make for a more rigid floor, which can enhance paddling or motoring performance. The external rigid inflatable keel gets that solid also when you fill it with air and provides sharper and more precise turning." Hogan said always happy to talk about his boat.

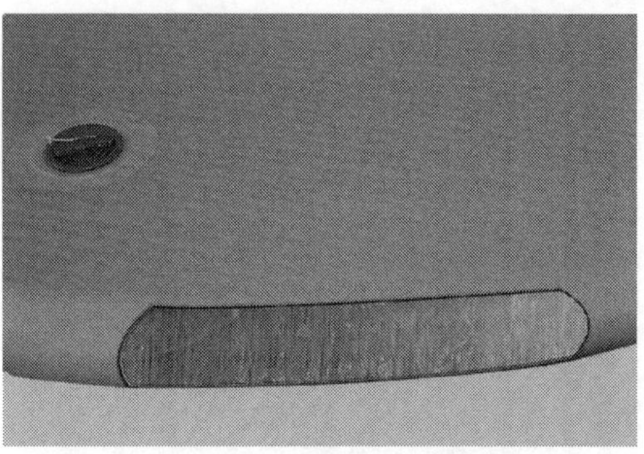

"So is that floor part of the boat or something separate like a drop in mat, maybe?" Dixon asked.

"The floor is a separate piece but you can leave it in and roll it up with the boat after you install it the first time. It secures to the transom but when you fill the boat up the sides hold it in place." Hogan said now starting to assemble his canopy.

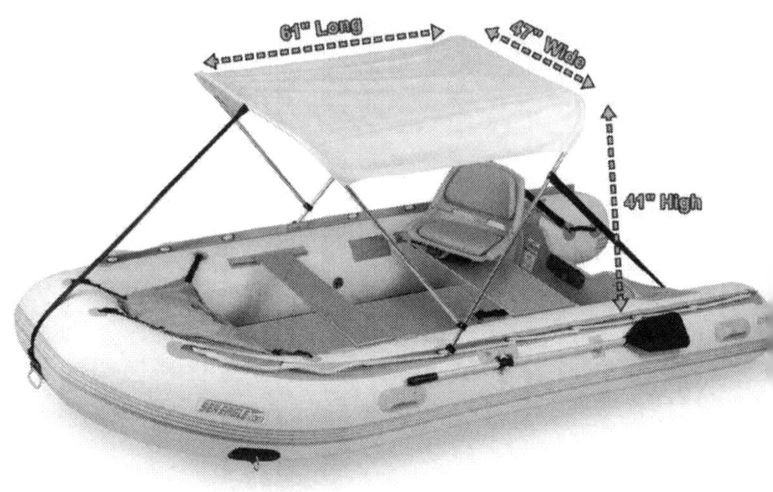

"Now ain't you fancy! Look at you, Hogan! Got you a nice comfy swivel seat to drive from and a sun awning to keep you cool! Now, Annie, that's the way to go fishing! Check out that nose bag he has got on the floorboard, Marylyn! The color matches the boat real nice, looks pretty waterproof. I bet that big pouch comes in real handy to keep your anchor and such in." Dixon said admiring Hogan's favorite accessory.

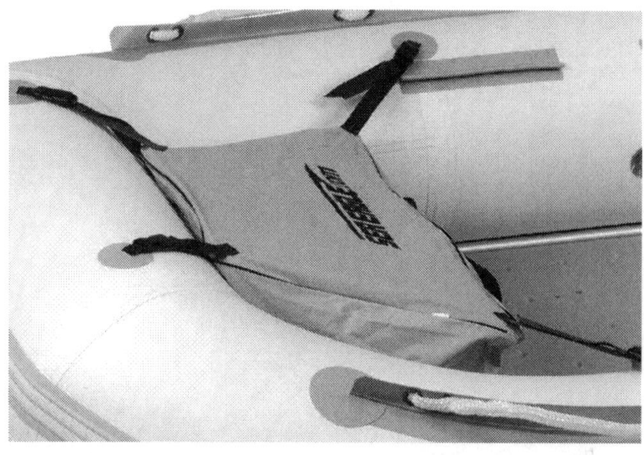

Bow Bag 10 6

"They make some nice backpacks also that I was meaning to outfit mine with but never got around to it. Being on a small boat or kayak makes you think more when you pack. If it isn't in something reasonably waterproof it's going to get wet.

Backpack

Dry bag

"I use a bunch of different sizes and colors of dry bags and when I go camping I put out what looks like a clothes line for a gear organizer and hopefully remember what I put in which color bag. That string system works real well for me when I am doing my setup base camp routine. I got flashlights and such in one, cook gear and clothes, etc., in another one and just go down the clothesline getting what I need and sealing them back up. If they get caught out in the rain, no biggie. When its time to leave camp I just grab the bags off the rope and put them back in the backpack or back in the nose cone and away I go. I don't lose things at the bottom of a backpack that way and pretty much know where everything is.' Hogan said.

"Sounds like a good plan. How long is it that you all are going to be gone for?" Marilyn asked causing Hogan to cringe and temporarily attempt to evade the subject.

"Not too long, they make a bigger size pack that also that fits a lot of their smaller boats. It has extra room for gear in it also but I had considered making me a big base camp pack out of one. You know for when it's only a short distance to a camp site and I want my big tent and awning and such. You can even pack that size in your luggage to fly with! Imagine being able to fly into the airport and get off the plane and pick up your Kayak or whatever at the luggage claim. That would be great!" Hogan said thinking how nice it would be to be able to do just that and check into a hotel or rent a car and go boating because you already had what you needed with you. Kind of gave a whole new meaning to the term "Bug Out Bag" he mused.

Hogan grabbed his trolling motor and battery in either hand and carried them down to install on the boat.

"It ain't everybody that can tote their battery and their motor at the same time!" Hogan said bragging on the fact that his Lithium Ion battery weighed less than half the weight of a normal lead cell one. At 100 Amp Hours and weighing just 30 lbs., the ReLion brand battery was a technological marvel.

"Well, you have either been taking your vitamins or that's an empty battery box you got there, Hogan." Dixon said looking incredulous.

"No, it's got a battery in it and it ain't a very light one, either." Hogan said sitting it down with some effort.

"Oh you got yourself some kind of small battery hid in that big box then." Dixon said with a smile thinking he had caught on to Hogan's alleged ruse of being super strong.

"No, it's a full size battery. It's just one of the latest greatest big investments I made in the technology world that makes my life easier but will last a long time." Hogan said opening the box up to show him the battery inside.

"I heard of lithium Ion batteries but I have never seen one that big before. What are you going to do when you run that battery down? I see you got a little outboard motor also so I guess then you will just be dependant on that until you run out of gas." Dixon said pondering if he could maybe cut himself a deal trading with Hogan for some of the gas he had in his car tank.

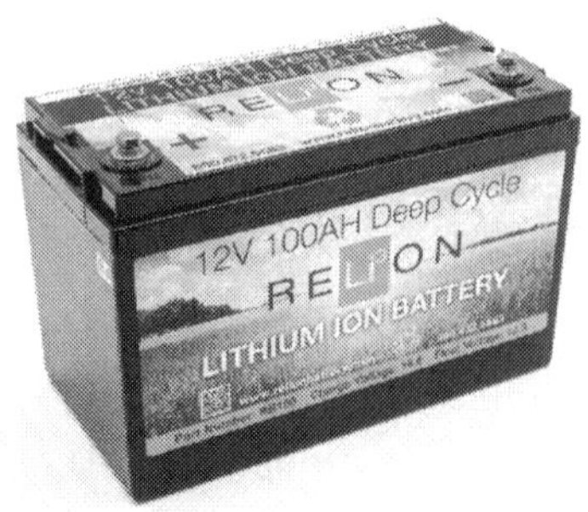

"A 100 Ah battery is pretty much over kill for what I would normally need for a day's fishing but I put a lot of thought into how I power my boat as well as various electronic devices needs when I am going long term camping." Hogan said.

"I also have a few ways to recharge that battery off grid. I can use an inverter off my car battery to plug in a high speed battery charger (special offer for my readers at end of book) but that requires gas for the engine though to spin the alternator. I do have considerable solar power capability though, with a very cool set of foldable panels." Hogan said opening the bow bag in his boat and removing what looked like a pouch and handing it to Dixon to inspect.

"That's pretty lightweight! You say this little solar package can charge up that big battery?" Dixon said handing it back to Hogan.

Folded: 13.25" x 7"

"Oh sure, no problem, and it can do it better than any other solar panels on the market that I know of for its wattage. They fold out bigger than you think, check this out." Hogan said quickly unfolding them.

Unfolded: 47.5" x 51.5"

"Now that's pretty slick, if you ask me!" Dixon said as he and Marylyn moved closer to observe and listen to what they were told were amorphous panels.

"Why choose an amorphous panel?" Dixon said knowing a thing or two about the differences in solar panels.

"Well for my application this type of panel outperforms crystalline and other thin film technologies in many real-world environments collecting energy in cloudy, shady, hazy environments where crystalline panels will not. I travel down a lot of shady creeks with tree over hang so I really prefer this type of technology. Both types of panels have their pluses and minuses but Power output is exceptional even in low light conditions. These panels fold very easily and are so compact I can even carry them in my backpack. The company that makes these panels was chosen by the military to make panels for them because of their unmatched durability. The manufacturer designed these for use in even the harshest environments and PowerFilm's proprietary processes produce a panel that works even after being punctured. There is a video on their website showing them shooting a panel full of bullet holes and then putting a voltmeter on them. The panel lost very little performance! That's the kind of rock solid dependability I want in a product that I have to depend on as much as I do with trolling motor recharging capability. That Relion battery of mine is rated at something like 20 years so paired up with these solar panels they will probably outlast the motor. I don't know though, that Water Snake Venom 34 lb thrust motor is made for both saltwater and fresh. You won't see that particular corrosion resistant model outside of Sea Eagle vendors, though. They chose this energy efficient motor as a great match for many of their boats."

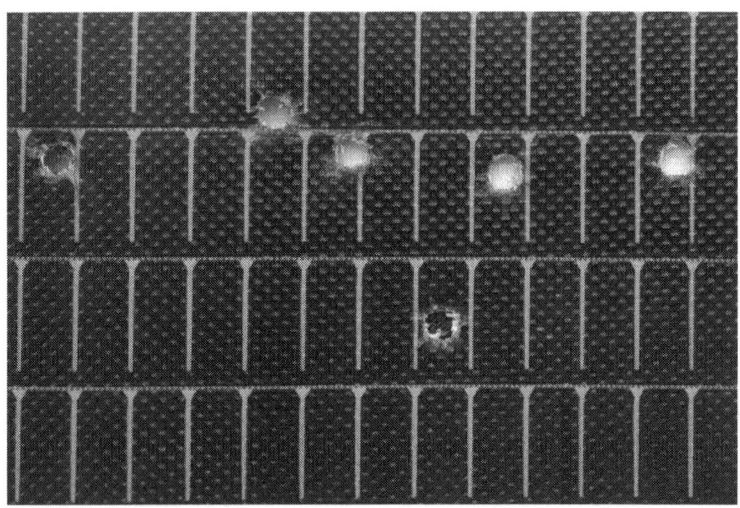

Damage to individual area shuts down the damaged area not the entire solar panel producing power after being punctured or scratched. This is Critical in potentially high-stress environments or applications

"Sea Eagle was the one that turned me onto Power Film's line of solar products, by the way. Boy, that was an education. Now foldable Solar Chargers are better suited for typically dry environments and must be dry when in use. For marine/wet applications, I was advised to reference Power Film's line of Rollable Solar Chargers. Now you might ask me why I didn't go rollable and that's a fair question. You see my education started when I was admiring a Sea eagle offering of a very cool setup. This is where you get into your size versus technology set up." Hogan said describing the neat craft that had caught his eye.

"Now that particular solar rig uses a special panel that PowerFilm developed just for a Torqeedo electric outboard motor. Notice I said outboard, we are not talking about a trolling motor here but something much more powerful that is equivalent to a three horse power gas motor. It uses a Lithium battery also that actually fits on top of the motor head and is much less powerful than the one I am using for my trolling motor by the way. They use a lower wattage panel with a very specific voltage output designed to match the needs of that brain board circuitry in the Torqeedo motor and battery. Now that system is cool and a good alternative to gas for a lot of power but I designed my system to run a trolling motor for long distances. You see that solar panel on the

Torqeedo doesn't extend your travel distance at all. That was an amazing fact that I didn't know until I talked to Torqeedo themselves about different applications. My setup gives me about a 25% increase in motor use travel time as well as I have that big amp hour battery so my system is actually much more efficient and way less pricy than that Torqeedo rig if I want to travel a long distance. Of course, I am giving up considerable power and speed but that isn't a factor I concern myself with. Mostly because I am not in a big hurry when I go fishing. I have a little gas outboard if I want to go faster with for sightseeing or whatever so I am all set. Now if I really wanted to get some speed out of this boat I can put up to a fifteen horsepower on this thing and fly around like I am going to the moon but that ain't my idea of fun. I like a more relaxing and less invigorating ride you might say." Hogan explained detailing why he thought his solar boat setup had many practical advantages over the more technologically advanced Torqeedo commercial setup for what he wanted to accomplish.

"So you didn't tell me why you ended up getting a fold up one and didn't get a rollup panel." Dixon said.

"Oh that's simple; those rollup panels are longer than fold ups. A rollup 60 watt panel is long and skinny at 86 inches long and won't fit on my canopy. My fold up panel is wider and only 51.5" long. While mine is not waterproof, it is very durable and water resistant. PowerFilm recommends wiping it dry if it becomes wet. The panel rides above the water on top of the canopy so I don't much worry about it." Hogan declared and started moving supplies to the bank to be loaded on the boat after he launched.

"So I take it that you are not worried about your boat getting punctured by some submerged tree limb or rock?" Dixon asked.

"Oh no, I am not worried at all. Of course that doesn't mean I am not safety conscious of sharp pokey things but I wouldn't say that I was overly concerned. If the grid was still up and the internet was still working I could show you a toughness video Sea Eagle made of a man beating pretty hard on the top and sides of this model boat's hull a bunch of times with both ends of a claw hammer and there was no damage or leakage to be noted. That's a pretty amazing test to video and put out for your customers. The bottom of the boat is even tougher. There is a 3" Rubbing Strake around the hull for extra protection as well as two layers of material on the lower tubes to afford it the greatest abrasion and puncture resistance. I will be floating around on that boat for many years to come with no worries." Hogan said confidently.

"I suppose you're totally right, I guess I never gave it much thought before but they use those kind of inflatable boats for search and rescue all the time and you always see the Navy Seals outfitted in full combat gear using them. They got to be making those boats these days really tough and durable for that kind of trusted dependability." Dixon said with new admiration for Hogan's boat.

"Annie, if you are ready to launch your Kayak, I guess we load you first." Hogan said noting Dixon and Marylyn didn't look like they had any intentions of leaving at the moment and pondered his next move of loading his boat with all that extra gear.

"I am ready; let's get loaded then." Annie said picking up her boat and carrying it to the water.

"That's amazing how that girl can carry that thing so easily." Marylyn said as Annie launched her boat.

Annie made a comical making a muscle movement with her arm and smiled back at the group. She then waded out into the river about ankle deep with her backpack and put it in as Hogan picked up a duffle bag and walked in about knee deep and put it in the front of Annie's Kayak.

"Would you please hold this line, Marylyn?" Annie said handing her the Kayak rope.

"Sure, wouldn't want your kayak floating off before you can get on. The river has a pretty good current going today, it appears." Marylyn said as she grabbed the line and stood watching Annie and Hogan pick up his boat from each end and carry it down to the river.

"I got the heavy end." Hogan said using his height and strength because he had already attached the bow bag and it contained about 35-40 lbs. of gear on top of his end of the boat.

"You are still moving it around easy enough though, it appears." Dixon observed giving him a compliment and wishing he was younger.

"Now for the fun part." Hogan said carrying the trolling motor and wading out in the water to hook it to the transom in the upright position after he had gotten it affixed. The battery came next and he connected the positive and negative leads from the motor to it.

"That's easy enough to do wading in during the summertime but getting in the water in the winter and then into the boat is not something I like. I have been threatening to get me a pair of hip waders for that season but I keep scaring myself thinking I will fall in and fill the boots full of water and sink like a rock. I have never messed with a pair of those but like everything else I suppose there are some insights I can get from somebody that uses them regularly to guide me." Hogan remarked as he grabbed his overloaded bug out bag and got it situated as Annie busied herself grabbing more gear and letting Hogan splash around loading it where he wanted it.

"You certainly have got enough tie down points on that boat with all those grab lines." Dixon said noting the boats 5/8" rope looped safety lines.

"Yea, this thing is probably impossible to flip, unlike a kayak but I am one for securing my gear down tight just in case. Those grab lines could help a swimmer like a life raft does but it gives you a place to hang on to if you're putting the boat through its paces in rough water also. This boat is proven to be seaworthy in most conditions but I don't want to try my inexperienced hand at any Class Three rapids. I am sure the boat could handle it but I don't think my nerves could. By the way, I think those tourist white water rafting trips are for the birds. I am not that crazy to think hanging on for dear life looks like fun and have no desire to do whitewater river running whatsoever." Hogan said now retrieving his shotgun from the front seat of his van.

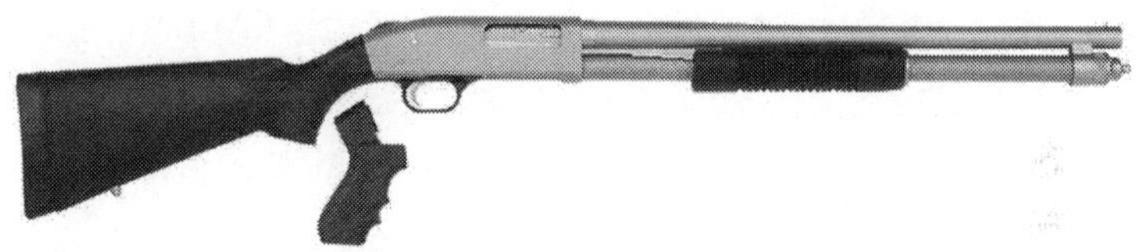

"Mossberg Mariner?" Dixon asked recognizing the Marinecote™ finish.

Mossberg provides shotguns to the U.S. military. They claim that *only* their Model 500/590 tactical shotguns fully meet or exceed the U.S. military MilSpec 3443 requirements for endurance, chemical resistance, drop tests, patterning, parts interchangeability and quality assurance.

"Let me see that shotgun, if you don't mind." Dixon said reaching for it as Hogan warned him it was loaded and gave it to him for inspection.

"Well there ain't no rust on it, that special finish really protects it, don't it?" Dixon said handing it back.

"Oh there has been rigorous testing that proves the Marinecote resists corrosion better than stainless steel. This finish is harder than ordinary gunmetal and provides the added bonus of greater resistance to wear and a distinctly smoother action. I take good care of my guns though and do regular cleanings." Hogan said loading it into his boat.

"Hey Hogan, if you don't want too much for them and have some extra shotgun shells, I would like to buy some. I have me a Mossberg hunting shotgun at home that needs some ammo. I have some cash or maybe you might want some gas in trade." Dixon offered.

"I can give you a few rounds no charge, I got plenty. What kind of rounds are you hunting?" Hogan asked.

"Pretty much anything that goes bang. I want to pay you something for them, though." Dixon argued.

"You helped them young bucks out with some fishing gear; I reckon I can help you out with some of the same sentiment. Take five boxes of whatever shells you need out of that ammo can sitting under that army blanket by the vans backdoor. Like I said, I got plenty of ammo... There is a mix of shells in there but if you want me to make suggestions as to what to pick maybe I can advise you on what to grab." Hogan said dismissively waving Dixon towards the side of the van while he tried to offload the two weighty buckets of beans and rice without showing how truly heavy they were to Marylyn or her husband's scrutiny. It didn't help that the sides were emblazoned with the manufacturers logo either saying "Emergency Essentials."

"We have got gas in our cars you might be able to use; we aren't going anywhere that I know of." Marylyn said noticing Hogan had hold of something pretty heavy in the back of the van that he was trying to get out. She saw it was two huge buckets then and began wondering what it was in them and worried if his inflatable craft could hold each ponderous bucket without sinking low in the water.

"What do you have in those? That stuff ain't going to put your boat over its weight limit is it?" Marylyn said unabashedly making Hogan flinch in an "oh hell moment" that he was finally caught moving substantial preps.

"We decided we would stay about a week so. Me and Annie decided if we were going to be gone that long that we needed bucket loads of bull shit you might say." Hogan said not willing to let on yet what exactly those five gallon buckets might contain.

"I could be here looking in this box all day Hogan deciding what I need to get. You better come help me out. I never heard of some of these manufacturers before let alone what it is I am looking at or using them for. You better help me choose. What the hell is an armored Brenneke slug used for anyway?" Dixon said digging around the steel ammo box.

"That's what I call an attitude adjuster round; they will go through the steel engine block of a car. You don't need any of those unless you plan on going to Africa sometime soon to hunt a cape buffalo or something. Here, get you some regular rifled slugs, buckshot, no 4 bird and a big twenty five round economy box of number 6 for an assortment." Hogan said grabbing several boxes and putting them next to a half full pillow case.

"Dang, Hogan, that's over 50 rounds you are giving to me, would you take a fifty dollar bill for all of it?" Dixon questioned.

"I would take it gladly if you got fifty in some smaller bills. I will only take that cash from you because I am short on any kind of funds whatsoever these days with no banking, as you well can imagine. I will do that deal with you, that is if you also take that bag of canned goods and a bag of rice and some advice Annie has for you without complaining too much." Hogan offered.

"Like I said I got money or barter Hogan, would a hundred do you for the lot, maybe a hundred fifty?" Dixon said seeing Annie go to get what looked like a huge bag of rice and beans.

"Hang on to your money; you are going to need it more than me. Tell you what, Dixon and Marylyn, how about you two doing us a favor by agreeing to do some house sitting for us while we are gone?" Annie said to the confused couple.

"What is it that you are proposing, Annie?" Marylyn queried.

"We weren't sure if you guys had any guns or not until now so we didn't mention an idea we had yet. I have moved in with Hogan for the duration of this problem and since we are going out camping on the river for awhile, we figured maybe you could do us a favor and watch the house and vehicles for us. You would be doing us a big favor guarding our stuff and we are willing to pay you a little bit for your trouble in food goods for doing it." Annie said.

"Well maybe we could do that, I don't know what kind of guards two old duffers would be for you to deter thieves, but I am interested." Dixon said.

"Are you interested, Marylyn?" Annie asked to which she got an immediate "yes" response from the woman.

"Me and Annie got to thinking about the situation around here, Dixon. You know one day the house next to you can be completely safe and then the next day there might be someone inside right next-door who wants to harm you. I don't mean that weird couple next to you. I mean simply everyone is going to be trying to do their best to be survivors now and you can never be sure how safe and secure your surroundings are from this point on. That's another reason for you to try to team up with those big old boys next to me for a bit. I don't know if they got any guns of their own or not but I am sure an extra armed citizen or two on their side would be useful to them. Particularly one nice well armed couple I know in possession of a trotline and the old style fishing skills to use it properly. It is going to get pretty dangerous around here because you'll have a lot of people in a relatively small area and you'll have higher demand for (very limited) resources. Now that the 'system' is gone, it is going to get a bit crazy. Might be good for you all if you can maybe find someone to help watch each other's backs. It might also be good if you were living closer to the river which just happens to be where we park our vehicles." Hogan said.

"Now that makes plenty of sense to me." Marylyn said with Dixon agreeing.

"Pretty soon the way we see it around here in regards to daily living, is that just plain survival will become an all day, every day task. Everyone is going to need to be constantly hunting, scavenging, gathering, finding information, looking for things and checking on things. Right now, you two can watch Hogan's apartment and our vehicles and keep an eye on that trotline you got from the apartment. Kind of guard the home front for both of us, if you know what I mean. If you're hanging out over here maybe you can get friendlier with the folks back here in these buildings and do the same for them. Kind of be like the neighborhood watch commander or something. I have no idea if anyone has firearms around here but I think not many do." Annie said.

"Well I don't know what to say to that kind offer but yes we will sure do it, Hogan... Annie be honest with me now. You are never coming back are you?" Dixon said regarding the pair more closely.

"Now what makes you say that? We are going to be back but since you will be around to guard the place it might be more like a month that we will be gone." Hogan said.

"Well giving us all that food and your house don't sound like you are coming back." Marylyn said skeptically.

"He didn't say he was giving it to us, he said we could just stay there for awhile to guard his stuff." Dixon offered.

"That's an awful long camping trip; you think that you're going to just live off the land?" Marylyn began.

"Oh I know better than that, we got plenty of food to see us through. If we get lucky and get a deer, you might see us back here for a visit and I will give you some venison." Hogan said loading the last of his gear.

"Go ahead and park your car, Annie." Hogan said indicating she should go to the apartment and walk back and then he would move his van.

Annie left and Hogan stood with Dixon and Marylyn on the river bank.

"Sounds like you're going to have the camping trip of your life, Hogan. You all be careful out there and watch out for hooligans." Dixon said as Hogan handed him some keys to the apartment.

"Oh we will, you do the same here. There is a propane camp stove with three canisters on the kitchen counter, feel free to use it and anything else you find in the house. Get Annie's key off her when she gets back to her apartment, I don't think there is much of anything left there that you might want but help yourself, you never know." Hogan said.

"You all try to come back in a week or two." Marylyn said already missing her new friends and starting to worry.

"No problem, we will try. We are going about 20 miles downstream but you might see us riding in one morning when you're out fishing." Hogan said with a smile not really planning on coming back by that soon.

"I guess if we don't see you in a month we will know you are truly gone." Marylyn said still wondering about Hogan's true intentions.

"We will be getting back here eventually, well let's put it this way. When we come back THEN we will be leaving for good. The plan is that we go on vacation now and wait on the roads to clear and for things to settle down around here some." Hogan said confiding in them.

"Well I hope and pray that they get the roads cleared up some in a month but you know things ain't going to settle down around here that quickly. Things will probably actually be much worse around here then. You know full well why I wanted more ammunition, Hogan, I bet." Dixon said being cognizant of the coming chaos and lawlessness they both expected.

"Yea, I knew what you wanted it for. I guess you could call me being either a chicken shit or a smart man for leaving and wanting to go on vacation now upriver for a bit. I don't know which one to call it myself, I don't really care. I know one thing though and that is we are going to go avoid some BS around here by moving into the woods for a short bit. I know the woods are going to be filled with gun toting fools also but I have got me a spot all picked out that is secluded and I doubt I will even see anybody at all. Hopefully, after a little bit of time passes, I can take my van out on the highway and go to my little farm in Alabama and start scratching in the dirt and growing me a garden." Hogan said wishing that he could be back home in his garden working on planting some things to eat later.

"I got some houseplants and a couple big pots of dirt for you on my patio that you can have, Dixon. Here is a pack of tomato seeds and herb seeds I was going to get around to planting but never did." Annie said handing a few small packages to Marylyn that she had remembered to grab when she went to park her car.

"Well we won't have any tomatoes for you all to eat when you get back but we will hopefully be able to show you some fine starts on some tomato plants!" Marylyn gushed as she received the seed bounty from Annie who in turn beamed her back a pretty smile.

"You two are some darn good people to be giving us this chance, don't you worry none about your stuff,

Hogan. I am going straight home to get my shotgun and me and Marylyn will move into that apartment as soon as you all cast off." Dixon said with a sly wink and then shook Hogan's hand.

"Well I guess then this is goodbye for now! Oh I hate to go like this... Be careful and catch lots of fish!" Annie said and hugged both the old people goodbye and went down to the river teary eyed with Hogan after he finished saying his own emotional farewells.

To hunt successfully, you must know your ground, your pack and your quarry.
--K. J. PARKER

7

Camping On The Hooch

The Chattahoochee River (often called the 'Hooch' by locals) is generally speaking, at least around here not that dangerous of a river. But Hogan knew in a SHTF situation almost everything is a threat to you. Oh it is easy enough to understand that in the city you have threats like gangs, angry neighbors and bad people in general etc., but the same goes for many parts of the woods. He also worried about possible pirate activity starting up on the river at some point. There were many other threats on Hogan and Annie's mind, like other campers desperation and lack of food, the lack of normal hygiene, any levels of contamination coming down river, theirs as well as others risk of injury just by chance meetings, being found, being informed on, being tricked by others, really more threats than most people ever consider to think about.

It was a new shocking reality to them and the relative seclusion they sought was the only thing that gave them any kind of solace to think about.

You can be hoping for the best and preparing for the worst but it's not easy to prepare for the consequences of the worst and the best of humanity being thrown together and the consequences of all them trying to survive differently during a disaster. Who was it that said "Our Generation is better prepared for a zombie apocalypse than for an hour without electricity." He bet it was someone that could only conceive of the dangers of this disaster from watching the TV show "The Walking Dead."

People like that had an unrealistic outlook as well as false expectations of what it would take to truly survive these days and times. For most people in the city, they had two choices: either to die in huge numbers, (which they will end up doing anyway) or to look for food and other resources in a way that looks the 'easiest' to them and that unfortunately becomes actually taking goods by force or theft from one another.

What Hogan and Annie were doing was trying to avoid the presence and demands of people in general and not get caught up in the mindless turf wars of controlling resources and the thievery and robbery to survive that was bound to happen.

Hogan was just using his trolling motor to pull Annie's Kayak along and he had left his cumbersome and noisy gas motor back at the apartment.

He had his eyes open and expected a surprise on the river just like he always did when boating but he hoped it would be a pleasant experience like seeing a deer or something. I bet the animals didn't know hunting season had just started and anything goes now. A lot of the wildlife around the parks was used to seeing people and would become easy prey at first, he reasoned.

"We will be at the "boat cave" shortly. I still think that name you came up with for the entrance is awful funny." Hogan said.

"It just seemed like it fit. I can't wait to see it in person!" Annie said excitedly.

"It is right up there ahead just on the edge of that bluff on the left." Hogan said pointing towards where the little inlet was hidden by some bushes.

"I am guessing that it is on the bank where that dead foliage is but you can't tell it's even there other than that." Annie said scrutinizing the shoreline.

Camping On The Hooch

"Looks like my camouflage is getting old and needs replacing." Hogan said spotting the golden brown dead vegetation and thinking he could have chosen better plants that didn't dry out so brightly to do the job with.

"Just reach over there and swing those bushes back like a gate or better yet just hold on to them and I will back up with the motor." Hogan said as Annie swung the gate out of the way as Hogan was backing away from it.

"Open Sesame!" Annie joked and then remarked how cool she thought Hogan's little scrub brush gate rig was.

Camping On The Hooch

Hogan guided the boat into the narrow little ditch like affair and they beached and dragged both the boats to shore.

"I hate this part; I need to rig me a string or something to that gate so I can pull it closed from here. I don't like fooling with brush over water because of poisonous water moccasin snakes and this is pretty muddy and leechy looking water if you ask me back in here." Hogan said not so much worried about a snake at the moment but cringing at the thought of emerging from the water maybe with several slimy blood suckers attached to him. Thinking about parasites of any kind on land or water, made him itchy and filled with dread about removing ticks or something like a fat leech from his body.

"Ugh! I hate Leeches! I am glad you told me about them! Is there any in there?"Annie asked looking at the murky water.

"No, but experience tells me to get in and out quick and have underwear on." Hogan said wading out into the swampy looking edge.

"Wait a minute, tie this paracord onto it if you can." Annie offered digging into a pouch on her bug out bag and throwing Hogan a 50 foot hank of green nylon cord.

"Thanks, I will give it back to you when we leave." Hogan said.

"I don't care about the cord; just don't stay out in that water long." Annie said watching the water get even muddier as Hogan walked along the bottom trying to keep the silt and the gumbo like red clay from sucking his boat shoes off.

Hogan messed with the brush gate and tried various methods of pulling it closed with the cord until he finally got it right and waded back to shore with caked shoes and a distinctive dirty waterline half way up his shorts.

"You're a mess!" Annie said looking at Hogan whose shins had an orange muddy tint and his thighs were covered in bits of dirt and floating twigs and such.

"Yea it's fun to have to wash off in the same crap you got on you. Gimme your canteen cup please, that will make it easier." Hogan said and sort of sluiced off with it after she gave it to him.

"It doesn't look like to me you got any leeches on you, thank God." Annie said watching to see if any of those twigs Hogan had on him wiggled.

"I am glad for that, I haven't seen any mind you but that water wasn't that low when I rigged that gate. Hopefully we will get some rain and raise the water level again." Hogan said.

"Do you want to unload the boats first or can we go exploring a little? I don't like to make camp without having a look around sometimes." Annie said picking up the 9mm rifle and its backpack of caliber conversions and ammo.

They decided to scout the area around the campsite before pitching the tent and Hogan led her up the sketchy trail to the bluff and showed her the unique overlook of the river and their proposed camp.

"That smoke from the city stinks really bad, I noticed coming up here to the top. I thought it was going to be worse once we hit the summit but it's not." Annie remarked as Hogan showed her this special place.

"I noticed that too... It's got me worried now because I remember my army chemical weapons training about heavy gasses concentrating in foxholes and such when the general ground at the surface is fine to breathe. We might want to sling my hammocks up here to sleep in and leave the tent setup down there." Hogan said pondering what gases from burning city debris and fuels might concentrate in low lying areas.

Camping On The Hooch

"You got hammocks? As in two?" Annie said never ceasing to be amazed at what Hogan had in his bag of tricks.

"Oh yea, I got two of the best selling famous ones on the market. They are Hennesey Hammocks, You might call them the industrial strength where-with-all of hammocks that reinvented the concept of hanging between two trees to rest. I use them for river camping mostly where it's hard to find a cleared space on the bank for a tent or when lightweight hiking a forest." Hogan said beaming his pride with a smile that he had the handiest dandy way that anyone could ever want to overcome this vexing problem of what they should be breathing at night.

"So you think we will be better off sleeping up here rather than down close to the water?" Annie asked trying to not consider just fog on an early morning could obscure the water on the river 10 feet in front of you.

"I have a hard time answering that question, before we came up here I was convinced it was safer below the peak because I was scared a wildfire might catch me snoozing up here at night. Now I don't know what to tell you. Let's wander and ponder on that notion for a minute while I show you my camps other features." Hogan said moving around a big boulder and showing her the skree of smaller rocks and big stones poised above the river about 50 yards from the trail to the camp.

"This pile of rocks is easy to collapse or you can just pick up rocks and throw a river full of headaches from here!" Hogan said.

"I can't envision why we would ever want to do that but point taken." Annie said to Hogan's unexpected boy like exuberance at playing at childish forts from his youthful upbringing.

"I bet you my bottom dollar that we won't have to speak to no one but each other for the next two weeks." Hogan said leading Annie down what he called the back path that went from the other side of the bluff and back down to the barely seen Indian trail to camp.

Both sides of the river contained for centuries a network of Indian trails before the white man came connecting trade routes and villages. The State Park offered these trails to tourists also but where Hogan had chosen to camp was many miles from marked trails.

The Chattahoochee River is where at least 32 ethnic groups came to live in the 1700s. They assimilated to become the Creek Indians by the end of that century. Two thousand years before then one of the earliest known permanent, agricultural towns, north of Mexico, was founded along its bank. Hogan wasn't the only one to ever like this place as a point of refuge.

Hogan and Annie set up housekeeping and bonding closer together and the land for the next week and a half before Hogan, tiring of commenting on and evading the occasional groups of kayakers going by they watched secretively from the bluff ceased and he declared a cautious holiday from playing "survival school."

He and Annie were going to take his bigger boat out and fish just for the fun of it.

He had himself plenty of time and absolutely no pressure to catch a fish so escaping the monotony of living on shore was a welcome respite. Hogan reminded Annie as they launched his Sea Eagle craft, that today should be just another day and to quit nervously clutching the TNW survival rifle so hard. He doubted they would need rifle or shotgun at all unless they saw a deer.

Evidently Hogan's thoughts of the deer population being driven this way with pressure from other hunters at the adjoining state parks were wrong. Their hunting efforts had produced nothing so far except some unwary squirrels and a possum Hogan had snared. Annie didn't particularly like being coaxed to eat it but it beat plain rice and beans and she had to admit didn't taste all that bad.

Camping On The Hooch

Hogan had commented a time or two if it was worth the time and the risk to go back to Mr. Wong's to find more soy sauce after getting semi addicted to it along with hot sauce to vary the diet after a few weeks. They did all right with their campfire cooking and basically were left alone in solitude.

They only had one encounter where a kayaker had hollered at Hogan seeing him on the bank and asking him did he have any food.

Hogan had hollered back that fish were free in the river if they were biting but he was sorry he hadn't had any luck today.

Today though was different, he wasn't subsistence fishing it was a contest of bragging rights casting for the big ones with Annie. It wasn't a matter of who caught the first or the most fish it was who got the first rod bender and lunker on the line.

Fishing tackle wise Annie was grossly mismatched as Annie wasn't the sportsman he was that had the age, opportunity and expense to try to catch some real gut buster sized fish.

The rules were simple in regard to species or ways of fishing to offset the differences in rod and reel sizes between them.

They each got two jugs they could bait for catfish and the same sized hooks, leaders and stinking fish bait to throw out in the current and shared equally in the wealth of Panther Martin lures and soft baits Hogan had in his tackle box. Hogan had the advantage here as they were fishing with his baits you might say but he gave Annie first choice to pick a synthetic or manmade lure to entice the game fish of her choice.

The deal was largest by species and not a singular fish because with the heavy Inland fishing rod Hogan had, it was evident he was only going to try for some sizable denizens of the deep.

They both put on their best fishing game faces and Hogan chose his artificial lure after Annie was done picking and said " Monkey dust" doing some weird magicians "prang" with his fingers towards the bait after he clipped it to the brass swivel on some ten pound test monofilament,

"You didn't happen to have any fish smell on that hand did you, Hogan?" Annie said not trusting him not to weight the game and bet in his favor by slipping in some fish attractant under his fingernails or something to get disbursed on the lure he had chosen.

"I ain't cheating, Annie! I swear to it. Tell you what, gimme three casts with this lure to loosen my arm up and I will change up and pick something else and you can use it if you want." Hogan offered.

Annie begrudgingly conceded that sounded fair to her but she was going to be watching him for tricks as the world class fishing tournament began.

Annie was the first one to reel in a whopper that Hogan felt hard pressed to compete with: a granddaddy trout.

After he had caught about three middling size largemouth bass that weren't going to win because of the biggest species caveat, something slammed his Secret weapon Panther Martin Tail Spinner that didn't feel like a large mouth. It peeled line off his reel and bored for the bottom.

"Big One!" came Hogan's immediate reply. The fish was strong and reminded him of a snook he had caught in Florida.

"Striper!" Hogan hollered jubilantly as the great fish tail danced across the sparkling waters trying to spit out the hook.

"It was a monster! It wasn't as big as some of the megalithic fishes he had seen other people catch in this river but it was his all time biggest score if he could land it on the boat.

Camping On The Hooch

Just when he was thinking about how to secure that behemoth of a fish it gill raked his line and got away.

Hogan had been in about mid sentence telling Annie she would never be able to win or boast about a fishing contest again when it happened and they both looked at empty water with their mouths open for a moment.

Annie burst out laughing at Hogan's bad luck as her bobber went under and a small crappie was found to be on the line.

"Hey we didn't include minnows as a species, Annie!" Hogan joked but was still grousing at the loss of that huge fish he had almost caught.

"I am glad that big fish didn't get on my line, it would of probably busted my rod in half. That rod of yours sure did hold up though. I had my doubts though for a minute, that big striper had your rod almost bent double." Annie said admiring Hogan's sturdy fishing rod.

Camping On The Hooch

"Boss gave me that Daiwa Harrier fishing rod and that fancy reel to me as a present for Christmas. He said I might know a lot about prepping but he knew more about fishing reels than I did and what could be caught around here as well as down on the Gulf. What I have here is a pretty much do it all setup that like my shotgun is built to serve many different purposes. That Daiwa Luvias 3000 is the smoothest spinning reel I have ever held. Everything about that spinning reel says it comes from a top shelf in their line of fishing reels crafted for exceptional strength and corrosion-resistance. . These are the kind of eye candy quality fishing tournament reels you might see off in the fancy locked wooden cabinet away from the glass display cases." Hogan said.

"That reel is smooth as glass and that magnetic oil feature instead of rubber seals I find amazing." Annie said.

"You know what is amazing? I am about to catch me another fish that size." Hogan boasted tying on a different unique bait made by Panther Martin.

Time was forgotten: they rose; they caught game occasionally; cooked and ate. They followed each other through the woods learning about each other as Hogan held class on what to do and when and the habits of nature he knew to observe.

Annie awoke to a marvelous sunny morning. She grabbed the 9mm carbine that was her constant companion and stepped out of the tent. It had rained the last couple days and they had moved closer to the river bank to watch the boats as well as avoid any lightning from the storm up on the ridge. Hogan was still asleep and she was quiet around camp so she didn't wake him.

She paused from trying to stir up the campfire ashes looking for glowing embers to start a new fire. She had seen movement from the corner of her eye from the trail by the bluff.

She froze after dropping the stick she was stirring the fire with and looked towards the trail. A shadowy form moved slowly in the woods and disappeared from sight.

Annie quickly moved to the camp stool she had her carbine leaned on and retrieved her weapon. She wanted to notify Hogan she had seen something but what was it? She was debating calling Hogan when she saw brush move where something had disappeared.

Annie shouldered her weapon and waited. A nice four point buck presented itself and she squeezed the trigger aiming just below the shoulder and it dropped like a sack of potatoes.

Hogan woke up instantly at the sound of the shot and grabbed his shotgun. He had sort of sat up in his sleeping bag grabbing the gun and then belly flopped over with the bag still around his waist and peeked out the tent flap.

"What's going on, Annie?" Hogan said from his vantage point a couple inches above the ground trying to scan the wood line where she was looking.

"No worries, Hogan. I just shot a deer!" Annie said jubilantly standing up.

"Way to go! I will be out to help you with it in a minute." Hogan said and then popped his head back into the tent.

"Ok! Hey it went down right off the trail by the bluff. I am going to go look at it." Annie called back.

"Ok, I will be there shortly!" "Hogan called from the tent as he worked on getting his boots on.

The deer lay motionless in the leaves next to the trail. Annie admired it for a moment and gave her thanks to the creature that had delivered itself so close to their doorstep.

Hogan wandered down the trail shortly and congratulated her on the clean kill. He wrestled with his need for more sleep and asked her if there was any coffee made yet. She advised him that there wasn't even a fire made yet and he suggested they go get coffee before cleaning the deer.

"That will give the carcass some time to cool so that's fine by me. I am going to just point that animals head downhill and slit its throat and let it bleed out." Annie said and pulled her sheath knife out to accomplish the task.

"Are you any good at cleaning deer, Annie?" Hogan asked watching her deftly accomplish the task.

"I have done a few, how about you?" Annie replied wiping her blade clean on some leaves.

"I have done my share. We can talk various techniques to get the task done easiest over coffee. I guess today is going to be another good day! That was quite a surprise to wake up to." Hogan said smiling as they headed back to camp.

"I was so lucky to see him! I didn't know what I was looking at until he stepped out. I thought about calling for you but I wasn't even sure what I was actually watching until he just walked slowly out into the open." Annie said happily recounting how she managed to get the scopes cross hairs on it.

"You did well, that ought to take away any doubts about 9mm you might of had." Hogan said knowing she was more familiar with high powered rifle rounds for deer hunting versus pistol caliber carbines.

"Oh I knew a 9 mm coming out of that rifle was potent. I was just worried if I was going to hit it. I don't have much range time with that gun, as you know." Annie said referring to the fact she had only shot it six times in practice.

"You didn't need no range time! You are a natural with that thing. You put six shots in two targets spread 30 yards apart. That shot you made was about 75 yards and if that was where you were aiming you were dead on target." Hogan said proud of her marksmanship.

"That's exactly where I was aiming. That rifle is a tack driver accurate piece of work, Hogan! Thank you so much for lending it to me." Annie said giving him a smiling hug.

"Wow, I ought to lend you my shotgun sometime. I could sleep in and play king of the campsite and you could wake me up when it was time for dinner." Hogan said kidding with her.

"Now you're being mean, I ought to make you clean that deer by yourself for that wisecrack." Annie said teasing him back.

"We ought to make Dixon and crew clean it. We could ride up to the bank with that pretty buck tied to the end of the bow of my boat and tell them "Behold the mighty hunters have returned!" Hogan said laughing. He said thinking that although he was joking, that didn't sound like such a bad idea.

"We should go check on them." Annie suggested seriously eying Hogan for confirmation.'

"I am thinking the same." Hogan came back with and suggested that they really should take the deer, hide and all back with them.

"Well if we left now it would take us about four hours to get to the landing. This is why we should have taken your gas motor but that is neither here nor there." Annie said thinking about when they would arrive and questioning Hogan about how long he thought the meat would keep in the oppressive heat that was soon to come later in the day.

"Do you want to take half this carcass to them?" Annie suggested.

"It would be good practice for us to try to cure the meat in a makeshift smoker here but if he has the Hulkster boys in tow by now we could maybe use that fancy grill of theirs to do a better job of it."Hogan suggested.

"I think you are right. I agree we should carry the apartment crew some meat today since we got lucky. How are we going to handle that? Do we let Dixon do the meat distribution?" Annie asked.

"I think that will be best, we told them we might be back to share and if they got the Hulksters working with them it might help prop up their leadership." Hogan suggested.

Annie figured that since checking on Dixon and Marylyn had come up they might as well discuss their impending departure for good out of here.

"Hogan, are you going to tell Marylyn and Dixon we are leaving soon?" Annie asked.

"Do you have any suggestions on how to do that? I am sort of at a loss on how to broach that subject let alone how we are actually going to just load up the vehicles and leave out." Hogan said watching the sticks and twigs they had thrown on the campfire catch and flame.

Camping On The Hooch

"No that last good bye tore me up, I don't look forward to the next couple. I know we can't do anything more for them than we have done but I hate leaving them permanently behind." Annie said sadly.

"Same here. Problem is we don't know how they are doing now. If they aren't getting along with the Hulksters, I figure they are barricaded in my apartment and not going out. There is not really any way of knowing what condition they are in." Hogan said hoping that the old married couple wasn't suffering much.

"We don't know what condition our vehicles are in, either. We are screwed if someone has stolen all our gas." Annie responded.

"I know, jeez coming up with plan ABCD, etc. is driving me crazy. I would probably be even crazier if I was hanging out with them back there rather than out here on vacation though. Well we knew this day was eventually coming, what do you want to do?" Hogan asked thinking he had enough so called vacation to last him awhile.

." I say we break camp and haul our crap back there and leave out for Alabama in the morning." Annie offered. Radio reception on the Hooch was spotty at best and from what they could ascertain over the last many weeks, the big cities were war zones, the President was hiding in a bunker somewhere away from Washington DC, the military was becoming factionalized as oath keepers, loyalists and various constitutionalists and nationalists vied for power and influence. Generally speaking, it was organized chaos from the top down as the populace reverted to another primordial century of comparable to the Dark Ages in cruelty and virulent death.

"I am for doing that if the vehicles still operate ok and we don't have any bad surprises when we get there. We could end up having our butts chased back here too. Have you thought about that yet, Annie?" Hogan asked thinking they already knew staying where they were at was not an option really. It was just too hard of living unless they made some major changes.

"Oh I have thought about that worse case scenario a lot, even if we can't get out of Atlanta by vehicle we are still so much better off than most. I ain't worried, Hogan. I think Marylyn and Dixon are doing as well as to be expected and the Hulksters are behaving and helping." Annie said.

"We took a big gamble, Annie, going on vacation like we did, I just hope it pays off in our favor." Hogan said reserving judgment for now.

"So what do you say? Break camp and tow my boat?" Annie asked.

"Let's do it!" Hogan said and they spent the next hour breaking camp before getting ready to cast off.

"The way that deer is sitting in the boat looks like I am trying to be a smart ass." Hogan said with a chuckle and a distorted grin.

"I admit that looks like a pretty much staged or posed deer we have there for a ships figurehead but it works!" Annie said grinning with Hogan about what an unlikely sight they were going to be with that deer as a boat ornament going up river.

They had eyed various ways to secure the dead deer and found just sitting it down in back of the bench and tying its legs around the front of it and the seat to be the most reasonable course of action.

Annie would sit next to Hogan on the captain's bench next to his seat in the back of the boat and the deer and the gear in the front would balance the load out. Hogan had tied the deer's head back by the horns giving it a zephyr car hood ornament look.

Camping On The Hooch

"Leave it to you to turn your boat into something that looks like a Viking long ship!" Annie laughed.

"It does sort of resemble one, don't it!" Hogan said as they cast off.

"I told you perfection takes time!" Hogan said as Annie used the Super Stik push pole to open the brush gate and push it back closed behind them.

"I am going to pull over here in a minute. As cool as that deer looks, let's not press our luck and throw a tarp over that thing. No sense us tempting fate or somebody's hunger with that thing." Hogan said ominously and pulled over towards the bank so they could hide the carcass. Once that was done, they resumed their trip up river without incident.

Camping On The Hooch

Several Kayak and motor boat camps were observed along the way, some with many members but no one challenged their right to navigate the waters.

That was a good thing in more ways than one because throwing that tarp over the deer blocked a lot of Hogan's vision as well as made it look like he was riding a giant Grinch sled with presents piled up in front of him.

When they got closer to the landing, Hogan said he had enough of trying to look around that lump and had Annie pull off the canvas.

"We might as well look spectacular!" Hogan joked as he resumed sailing his alleged Viking ship with a stag figurehead.

"Guess who is on the beach, Hogan!" Annie cried as she peered around the slightly bobbing deer's head.

"Hot damn! I see them up there waving their arms off . HEY DIXON AND MARYLYN!" Hogan shouted as Annie joined in hollering her own greetings to the couple.

"Watch out for my bobber!" Dixon called pointing out about mid river in front of him.

"What the hell is that? A buoy of some kind?" Hogan asked Annie.

"Looks like a giant bobber to me! I saw one of those things before! It's an ice chest!" Annie said as they neared the bank.

"We got the end of the trot line on it!" Marylyn called back.

"Well, I'll be damned." Hogan said as he looked at the improvised float.

"I gave him that cooler one Father's Day for a joke gift but he always liked it. Now it has a new use." Marylyn said as Hogan killed the motor and raised it up out of the water to clear the bottom as he got ready to land.

"Wish it had a beer in it for you, Hogan, but we're all out." Dixon said wading into the water to shake Hogan's hand and welcome him back.

Marylyn waded in also and they shoved the heavily laden boat to shore laughing about comments regarding Hogan's extra crew member boat ornament.

"You doing all right?" Hogan asked looking into the couple's tired faces.

"We are getting by. We sort of got them big boy neighbors of yours working with us. Got one of them pulling security and supposed to be watching us and this trotline over there." Dixon said pointing back towards the apartment buildings.

"He will probably go tell Nimrod and all them Hulkster boys will be down here. Did you plan on sharing that deer, Hogan?" Marylyn asked looking skeptical.

"It is you and Dixon's deer. Do what you want with it but we want some of the back strap for dinner." Hogan said reserving some of the choice cut for themselves.

"I shot it!" Annie said proudly and received hearty congratulations.

"Here come the Hulksters." Dixon said and went to talk to them.

In a few moments, two young men came down and carried off the deer back to their apartment where they were supposed to start cleaning it.

"Those two been deer hunting before but don't have any guns." Dixon confided.

"Is our stuff ok?" Hogan asked glad to be able to hurry up and ask that question and wondering what Dixon had said to the group that made them not want to stick around and socialize.

" Oh your vehicles are fine! Just as you left them. Told you we would look out for you." Dixon said with pride.

"What did you say to Nimrod that got him and some of his boys to go home?" Annie asked noting the odd behaviors.

"Oh, they are good boys but they aren't used to thinking for themselves." Dixon began before Marylyn cut him off.

"Actually what they are, is a group of Larry's in search of a Moe! Dixon has fun bunching them up when he wants." Marylyn said before allowing Dixon to continue.

Dixon chuckled and said that they were like a bunch of chickens. All you had to do is throw a little scratch feed in one direction and you could get the whole bunch moving in that direction.

He advised everyone he just told Nimrod to get ready to clean, guard and cook the deer and he had taken charge and grabbed everyone except the two boys that had carried the deer off to do all that.

"He did that with two squirrels last week he shot." Marylyn said chuckling.

"Ha! They are easy to mess with but I consider it being efficient. They do the group effort or team thing well." Dixon said smiling wickedly.

"Well, you know there are more Indians in this world than chiefs." Annie said smiling.

"That is a lot of mouths to feed." Hogan said wondering how they were managing to get by.

"So far we are doing ok. They all had a bunch of protein powder and supplements and stuff and they been living on that and the fish we catch." Marylyn said.

"There are a few wild greens around here I remember eating from being a boy and me and Marylyn have been adding them to the pot. We are all starving but we are eating." Dixon said.

"Me and Annie aren't hanging around. We decided it was time to make the big trip and are going to be taking off." Hogan said solemnly.

"Dang you just got here." Dixon objected.

"You can stay at least a da,y can't you?" Marylyn said looking upset.

"No, I think it will be better to go now. We are going to pack the vehicles and hang around an hour or so and get moving while we have lots of daylight to travel. Its only 3 hours to where we are going and Hogan is worried about his stuff." Annie said helping break the news of their departure.

"Well, you will be home way before sundown then if you don't run into any problems on the road." Dixon said looking a bit crestfallen they weren't going to stay around long for a visit.

"Wow, three hours by interstate isn't that far if the roads are clear enough to drive normal speeds." Marylyn said studying them.

"Hopefully we can do 65, if not who knows as long as we get there. Hey, if gas gets flowing again some kind of way maybe we can visit each other." Annie said and then regretted it.

"You give us your address before you go and maybe we see each other someday." Dixon said not really knowing what to say. Everybody knew that was a slim to none chance of ever happening.

"Yea we will do that. Hey Dixon walk up to the parking lot with me while I get my van. I want you to go tell Nimrod that Hunters choice says we get the back strap tenderloin. You sure them boys know what they're doing cleaning that deer?" Hogan said.

"Oh yea they can do it just fine. Two of them goomers were studying at the Atlanta Culinary Institute. Imagine that! We got would be apocalyptic food chefs with some talents in cooking. Not much they can practice on but fish." Dixon said as they left Marylyn and Annie behind to talk and guard the gear.

"Get them to try their hand at that clay baked fish thing. You know the one where you use real clay to coat the fish and bake it in the coals like a pot." Hogan suggested.

"Now that's an idea, I forgot about that bit of wood lore. I have been teaching them things best I can on what I call country living but we got a ways to go yet." Dixon said stopping to show Hogan the garden he and the Hulksters had dug up.

"How's you and Marylyn's health doing? Are you two holding up ok? Wow, Dixon, you have done a lot of work here! How hard was it to get them jackasses to dig all this up?" Hogan said looking at about a 200 x 15 foot swath of dirt.

"That ain't the only garden around here, there are two more and they are all basically community gardens with a few private sub sections." Dixon said with a knowing grin.

"What are you using for seed?" Hogan asked incredulously.

"Well pretty much a little of this and a whole lot of that. You see more folks have tried to grow themselves tomatoes on their back porch around here than we thought. Got a lot of green thumbs living around here and I will tell you more about them later. Most of them patio gardeners always bought transplants to grow in pots but a few people have seeds of this or that from trying it that way too. When me and Marylyn went to get them pots from Annie's apartment, we started studying what was on everybody else's patio and came up with a plan. The first thing we did was carry a mess of fresh fish we had caught over to the Hulksters as a means to call parlay. I told them me and Marylyn had some business to discuss. That was quite a surprise to them, what surprised them even more was I was toting my shotgun and Marylyn had her Police special .38 revolver stuffed in her waistband with the handle butt hanging out."

Dixon said describing what was called the first official meeting of the Hulkster club.

"Hang on a minute, Dixon, and stand around and talk to me a few minutes before we get around them boys. I want to hear more of this story first. So what did they think of you all open carrying guns at first?" Hogan asked very curious of the athletics boys reactions to a shotgun carrying old man and a gun carrying wife walking up to them and saying "here's some fish" let's parlay like an old western movie depicted settlers trading with Indians.

"The guns made them nervous and one of them asked were we having any trouble but mostly they acted like I just met them on the beach for the first time. I told them about our plan to get them to help me set out and guard the trotline and that I was a good fisherman and provider if luck and fate blessed me and Marilyn. They could see for themselves that fine mess of fish I gave them was a good catch but not enough for all of us to eat our fill and I needed some protection from those that might want to eat those and had none for themselves or even a means of catching any." Dixon explained.

"That shouldn't of been too hard to sell them on that notion, we discussed that earlier." Hogan said.

Camping On The Hooch

"You were right, Hogan. They saw the sense in that real clearly right from the get go. They agreed to stand night watch on the trotline as well as escort me and Marilynn around as need be as backup security." Dixon said.

"Well to make a long story short, you remember I told you me and Marylyn got to studying who had vegetable or herb plants on their balconies and patios... I told Nimrod we needed to start a company using my brains and his muscles." Dixon said chuckling.

"You didn't! What did he say to that?" Hogan said in true co-conspirator fashion.

"Well he listened and he agreed and we started the Acme Protection Service. Him and the boys call it "apps" for short like a program or something that goes on a phone or computer and me and Marylyn call it "Apes" like a primate you're toilet training to go on a newspaper." Dixon said with a loud guffaw.

"That's funnier than hell! So what do you have the Grape Apes doing these days to keep them busy?" Hogan asked snickering.

"Well, I grabbed me a gaggle of goons and went soliciting for our new business door to door but that didn't work out too well. You see Me and Marylyn as the spokespeople for the new company would go knock on a door we saw that had the growing things on the porch and introduce ourselves. We would say "Dear Sir or Madam, nice to see you today... We want to tell you about a cooperative we started regarding vegetable plants and protection. Well I know you are in a hurry so I won't list you many details but it was hard enough to get someone to open the door to us as old people and when they did and saw our guard dogs with us they thought we were on an extortion mission or something. One woman with a big tomato plant on her patio slammed the door in Marylyn's face and told her to just take the plant and don't hurt her after seeing them stick wielding boys. Well scaring the hell out of folks wasn't our intent so we changed tact and called a meeting of the apartment complex which wasn't easy to do for obvious reasons like not being able to print flyers and already freaking people out by knocking on doors unannounced but we eventually managed it." Dixon said remembering what a chore that was.

"I went down and busted in the complex business office and at the appointed day and time any resident that was aware of the meeting and wanted to come, appeared there. Marylyn, Me, and the boys all put on our Sunday best to go to the meeting. By the way, what some of them boys think is Sunday best might surprise you. Anyway, I got up there and I put the bully pulpit on them." Dixon said.

Author note: A **bully pulpit** is a conspicuous position that provides an opportunity to speak out and be listened to. This term was coined by President Theodore Roosevelt, who referred to the White House as a "**bully pulpit**", by which he meant a terrific platform from which to advocate an agenda.

"Gain, There is nothing to be gained here, Hogan. Only a chance to live in a more civil society by choice and cooperation. People need structure be it from religion, politics, threats of retribution or criminal penalties or whatever. Structure is the key, they seek governance and direction and a peoples movement is sometimes called a grassroots agenda. It was very simple to lay it out and not get shouted down with all that muscle I had in back of me to say "Listen up folks". You are going to die, we are all going to die if we don't cooperate and try to do something to help ourselves. Now anyone that got worried when we tried to go door to door to talk to you, don't worry. We are not trying to strong arm you into any decision. The reason the meeting was called was because no one should have any fears of growing a garden and being robbed and one Dixon P. Stone was here to get them to sign up for the solution! I told them all young and old we had to get us up a seed inventory and get it into the ground here and now. I explained to them that anyone who didn't want to be a member of the Co-Op didn't have to be but respect its rights and assist when they could. I think I got everyone listening closer and paying attention when I asked if anyone had thrown any rotting fruits or vegetables out within the last few days because the CO-Op needed the seeds to plant. Once they started seeing the daylight to that way of thinking, the rest was easy." Dixon said commenting on how he had motivated everyone to start raising seedlings and digging up dirt.

"You still haven't told me what you are using for seed or planting?" Hogan said thinking Dixon must have sent the Hulksters out to loot some seeds.

"Well that remains a problem but with everyone digging in the garbage cans for rotted fruit and Marilynn and her garden society teaching everyone how to save seeds, we can make a crop. Half that crap won't grow I know and I have no idea how some of that tropical stuff is going to manage but the thing is we got it in the ground if it is a seed and every apartment in this complex has a diversion growing or tilling dirt here. What they do outside the complex is their business as long as they don't bring trouble back here. 90 days to harvest is a long time to live on nothing. However a week of hope is worth a priceless treasure if it's shared. I did need to remind a few hold outs that other neighborhoods and people were likely organizing the same as us in order to survive and that I doubted it was raising a garden they had on their mind over raising hell." Dixon said painting the picture that Hogan had missed while on vacation.

"Damn man, you make me wish I had stayed around here longer or come back earlier. I could of maybe helped you with that organizing maybe. That's what I use to sort of do, if you remember right." Hogan said trying to take in all the amazing progress the old man and his wife had accomplished since him and Annie had been gone.

"You would have probably just got in the way. You had no plans on staying here, Hogan. You don't have any now. Me and Marylyn no sooner said hey to you when you and Annie started reminding us that you were leaving the next time we saw you. You got a place here if you want it, Hogan, you know that." Dixon said already knowing the response.

"From the bottom of my heart, I thank you my friend but this place is not for me. I guess Marylyn is telling the same story to Annie; She might want to stay here now because this place is closer to her home state and family. When we were on the river, I kind of convinced her that there was no more hope of ever seeing them again but I might have been wrong. If you managed to pull this apartment complex together to pull as one to survive then there is more love and miracles in this world than I thought." Hogan said patting the wise old man on the shoulder.

"Shit Hogan, quit being such a whiney idiot. Take that beautiful girl and haul ass fast as you can to what you know is better. If I were a younger man and had the knowledge you have, I wouldn't have even came back here. You think them modern society folks just quit thinking and looking out for themselves because this old man told them it was a good idea not to? They can't handle what's going on daily let me tell you and do the stupidest things believe me no matter how educated and liberal they are supposed to be. A few of them, not all mind you, are already sowing the seeds of discontent and being bitchy every way they know how to be still living in their selfish little worlds. It ain't been no touchy feely everybody getting along after the couple speeches I gave, not by a long shot. That's why I told you Hogan, you might have gotten in the way around here. See I was raised around moon shiners that had their own mob and way of influencing people to remain silent and helpful. A few folks needed an attitude adjustment you might say to know not to steal or threaten folks." Dixon said thinking that no one in his Acme protection plan would have been worried about leaving a pie to cool on their kitchen window sill if such a luxury ever existed anymore because a beat down of some sorts wasn't far away for the perpetrator if caught.

"It sounds like you got all your bases covered, hell you got people probably sharecropping for you by now." Hogan said with a laugh to which at first Dixon took offense but saw the humor in it.

"If you just want to get your van and not play with the boys yet you can, Hogan." Dixon said resuming their trip to retrieve the vehicle and him see about how the carcass was being cleaned.

"Go check on them and see how they are making out with that task. I will send Annie and Marylyn back up here shortly to get her car." Hogan said waving to the group of boys skinning out the deer but deciding rather than mingle just yet, he would make sure his vehicle was operable and get his gear off the beach while they were distracted.

'Many men go fishing all of their lives without knowing that it is not fish they are after.' Henry David Thoreau

Traveling Dangerously

"Holy Hell! Now is definitely not the time for us to be getting ourselves caught up in this traffic jam crap. Are all these crazy people evacuating from towns close by or is it that everyone is trying to get somewhere all at once?" Hogan thought to himself.

Annie had been following behind Hogan's van closely and he had finally managed to get them maneuvered into the left hand lane with a lot of cussing and trouble with other drivers. It was a good thing that he had been on this little stretch of highway before, because both of his previously planned on right lane exits he had wanted to take had been clogged.

Hogan had followed this mad card chase for survival longer than he had wanted to and he was looking for the lane exchange turn off to go back the other way. The chain reaction of a wildfire had begun. Crippling drought conditions and unchecked fires from surrounding communities were sparking blaze after blaze across six states in the South.

He strained his smoke irritated eyes looking out the window ahead trying to get a handle on exactly where this latest fire was at in relation to the road. As the fire storm approached, a piece of untouched ground somewhere close to the next exit it announced itself with a roar and a white hot light appeared on the horizon to his right.

Big migrations of fleeing people and cars were trying to all speed in one direction as the fire spread through the surrounding towns and the area. The fire was burning so hotly and so quickly that many of the evacuating residents had little time to escape with their lives, much less gather their belongings. Those who were preoccupied with packing to flee were caught unawares of the fatal danger of their tardiness. People became mindlessly panicked as smoking embers began falling in town near the propane plant.

The wind took the hot floor of the simmering forest and threw it into the air where it gained momentum by catching fire to the boughs of bigger trees. Pine sap heated quickly and hissed as it reached a boiling point. Wildfires move quickly. When it's hot, dry, and there's a lot of fuel, it can take just seconds for them to spread. Many people and animals would not escape this fire today.

Flames had roared on either side of the exit not far from the last road he had passed. Hogan was torn between wanting to have his window up or down as the smell of smoke and a roar like the "the sound of a storm at sea" assaulted his senses.

Finally! There it was, the crossover point he had been looking for and he and Annie headed back to the less trafficked northern lanes away from their objectives. Hogan eventually went about 40 miles out of his way and got on a more southerly eastern route eventually heading for the panhandle of Florida. There would be no going home to Alabama for now, at least not this way and probably for some time to come. Plan B was officially in motion. It didn't matter much to him how he managed it, but he was going to try to follow any road he could find that went ever eastward to the coastal waters.

A couple of hours driving should get him to the ocean eventually and he could figure out where exactly that might be as he went. Hopefully, there would be no more great fires to contend with and detour around. Once he got close to the Florida line he had his pick of many rivers and creeks that could also get him there if the roads got impassably bad.

His gas was holding up good, he had a bit over a half tank left and there was hardly any traffic at all on these back roads he was taking. He couldn't hear crap on his radio that helped him ascertain whether or not for him to expect anymore fires so he was mentally just seat of the pants navigating you might say. He knew that hopefully if he drove far enough East or South he should bump into some familiar territory and know where he was at but right now he was lost.

He eventually pulled over by the side of the road and got out to talk to Annie about what it was they were doing now that the fire was far behind them

." Annie, I have been thinking about the best way to approach the Florida line from here but I am a bit confused until I get to see some better land marks. Let's take a few minutes looking at this map and maybe see if we can guess where exactly it is that I have gotten us to so far." Hogan said pulling out a rumpled road map and trying to find his estimated starting point.

"Hogan, are we heading straight into Florida to stay or are you going to be trying to find your way back home to your house in Alabama?" Annie asked confused as to what it was he was attempting to do.

"I am thinking that we are pretty much stuck going to Florida and staying for awhile. That fire prevented me from going the few regular routes that I knew to go back that way. I think now the best thing to do would be just keep driving south east until I can recognize something or get directions. This road that we are on now as far as I can see isn't listed on this map or it's called something else that's not marked here. I haven't seen any road signs or highway markers for awhile, have you?" Hogan asked.

"Not since we turned around and you headed this way. Hogan, I want to thank you so much for turning around when you did. I have never been so scared or so glad in my life get off a road or out of a traffic jam. Most of the time I couldn't tell if we were heading towards a fire, going by a fire or the fire was chasing us." Annie said securing her wind blown hair under a camo ball cap.

"Me neither, that was a pretty scary ride but I wasn't leaving anything to chance. I was looking at taking the dirt median also. Anyway, we made it through ok and it looks like it is just a matter now of getting ourselves un-lost from here and back on our way." Hogan muttered as he went back to his befuddled map reading.

After a few minutes of trying to get their bearings, they began to assume that pretty much any part of the panhandle would be ok to come out at eventually and they set off down the road once again.

In about an hour or so of driving, Hogan began thinking that he knew exactly where it was they were at. Well more or less anyway and he settled in for a more leisurely calmer drive with lots of signs helping point him towards the beaches. When his instincts about the strip road they were on were confirmed not long after seeing a sign or two he turned after about fifteen miles and headed for a deserted stretch of coastal highway he had been on before. This was the road less traveled most of the time and he didn't see any cars.

Hogan pulled off the road after going several miles down the highway and then exited into a small residential area and parked between two billboard signs.

"Annie, this is part of the entrance to the estuary that comes out not too far from St. Joseph Peninsula State Park on the Gulf of Mexico across the bay from Port St. Joe. We are going to call this home for awhile." Hogan said surprising Annie that this was indeed the end of their journey for awhile.

"This is not what I expected at all, it looks like the end of a canal or something." Annie said thinking coastal meant ocean.

"Well this is a canal of sorts but you can get out on the big water from here. Locals use it for Kayaking. What we are going to do is unload our junk here and I guess scatter our cars a distance apart back out on the road like we are broke down or something. That way anyone coming down here won't think we just launched and might still have gas in the vehicles or possibly mistaking us for a kayaker coming back from fishing to rob maybe." Hogan said having worked out a bit of a strategy on the way here.

.

"That sounds reasonable, so now we have to find us a camp somewhere for tonight. Question is what are we going to be doing tomorrow?" Annie asked.

"That is sort of hard to answer. From this point on I don't know very much at all about the coast except that this or that should be over there off in a general direction. We will make do and fish and hunt until we decide where home is going to end up being for the summer. We are doing good and still have a month's worth of food, maybe we will just hang out and camp for a few days and decide what is next." Hogan said when confronted with the realization and fact that this was but the beginning of their journey and that he didn't know where this journey was going to end up at.

Annie and he conferred and decided to do just that for the following week. Just camp and leisurely pass the days exploring the coastline. They saw few other boaters but they made sure that they camped in obscure out of the way places. They just played nomad staying close to shore and to themselves, carefully and warily watching the water and the beach for signs of danger or an opportunity.

Not all dangers however, were visible to the eye as they were about to find out. Not all things could be seen even if you knew where to look. You also needed to know how to look.

9

The Great Reunion

Hogan pushed his boat off the beach and fought the light waves coming from the ocean until he got out far enough away from shore to jump in it and motor it out. Annie was already launched and paddling her kayak further out on the sparkling blue water waiting on him to join her. She said she preferred today to enjoy paddling for awhile rather than be towed or riding with Hogan. Hogan said he might also try to row his boat with the oars for awhile later but for now he would just as soon set the trolling motor on medium speed and sit under his canopy and ride.

They had made it about six miles paddling and motoring up the coast when Hogan pointed out a peninsula ahead that they needed to make for.

"What's over there?" Annie said floating in her kayak next to Hogan's boat.

"A long time ago I was looking around on the internet at big coastal acreage land with a client. He asked me if I knew about where a particular parcel might be located at because I frequented this coastline doing some fishing and camping and I guessed that it should be roughly around this location. I have never been to the property before but it should be around here somewhere. There wasn't anything built on the beach side of it the ad said but there was a caretaker's house and some big metal buildings inland. Looked like a lot of scrub oak woods on 700 acres with not a lot of accessible shoreline. That might be that same property up there, it's too far to see from here any details." Hogan said looking ahead.

Six miles today was pretty good traveling. There was no way they could of even hauled a ¼ of their gear and food hiking that distance let alone do it way before dark. Annie was fit and the kayak glided effortlessly at a pace she could never have walked however. Hogan kidded with her once or twice going over to the point by turning his motor on high and lounging back in his seat with his feet up and she struggled to keep up.

"There is a lot to be said for solar power and electric trolling motors!" Hogan had joked.

He had seen other people solarize their Sea Eagle boats with everything from do-it-yourself low wattage battery tender panels to the full blown commercial Sea Eagle Torqeedo Package.

Hogan had told Annie they would have to see about constructing her something to attach a trolling motor on her 370 model. He had seen the company do it on the more expensive 385 but he wasn't sure about modifying hers. Annie said that was the least of her worries because for one they didn't have an extra motor and battery and besides she got great joy in paddling hers just the way it was.

Hogan agreed and said they didn't have an extra solar panel either but he could have charged her up also in a day or two depending on battery size.

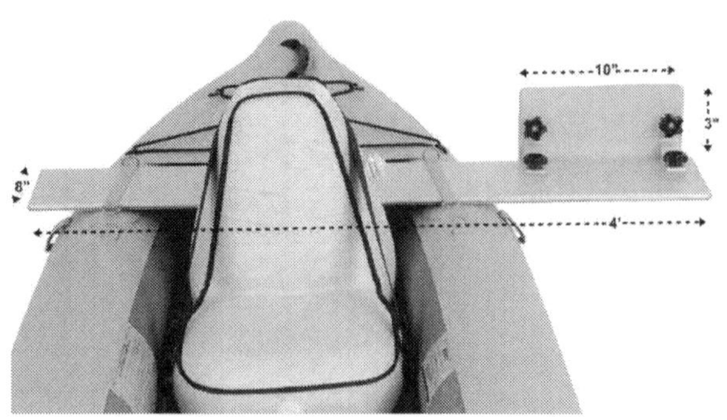

Motor mount

They got close to shore and started following its contours towards the little peninsula. As they progressed, Hogan slowed way down as some wisps of wood smoke made their appearance from the woods lining the shore up ahead. Annie motioned towards her nose she could smell food cooking and pointed to the shore and then off towards the bay indicating should they stay close to investigate or get further out on the water so they didn’t surprise the campers.

They were almost right up on rounding the point so Hogan decided to just to proceed cautiously and put his shotgun across his lap as Annie loosened the holster strap on her pistol.

Hogan saw a road heading in from a small beach and as he was passing it, suddenly stopped and put his trolling motor into reverse and waved Annie over pointing.

When she got close, he whispered that he recognized that trailer and that it was one of those neat Tetra Pod boats he had told her about.

"Wow, that's pretty cool. I can see what you mean about it also being a survival trailer now." She whispered back as Hogan looked around the area for signs of life while deep in thought on what it might be doing there.

"Could it be? What would be the chances of that actually being Sam's boat?" He speculated.

"Probably it was just someone who had one like it but those kinds of boats were relatively new on the market and not a lot of them to be seen around these parts. Sure it had to be someone else, Sam and Lori were most likely happily bugged in back at home in Alabama but the brush fires could have sent them this way." Hogan mused.

"Wouldn't it be great if his old friends were here?" Hogan thought and whispered his speculations to Annie who hoped he was right but that didn't change the fact they couldn't be sure and be cautious.

After a few moments of hesitation and listening Hogan called out "HELLO THE TETRAPOD!" and waited on a response. He called out again as they slowly proceeded forward towards the wood smoke up shore and was rewarded with a shout back after a long pause.

"Is that you, Hogan? Can that be my buddy?" The voice called back and pretty soon three figures appeared from the woods to a little shore.

"Yea, it's me you old Pirate! Now ain't this a coincidence! Hey, Lori girl!" A jubilant Hogan called back.

"It's them Annie! It's really them! How lucky can we get? I can't believe this!" Hogan said beside himself and smiling with glee as he motored his boat towards them waving and hollering.

"I see that!" Annie replied and paddled furiously to catch up with Hogan who was heading for the excited trio.

"You all be careful of the stingrays getting out!" Sam called back as they headed towards the beach.

"What sting rays? WHERE?" Annie asked looking on both the surface and down in the shallow water around her.

"Oh there is probably one around somewhere, just poke your paddle in the sand and they will take off and move." Lori called back.

"Hogan, I can't believe that is you! Mind the stingrays; we don't call this place Stingray Point for nothing. They won't bother you none unless you step right on one but chances are you will scare a few up." Sam said as Hogan and Lori carefully put in and Hogan beached his boat.

Annie parked her kayak on the shore and followed Hogan.

After Hogan got done hugging Sam and Lori and getting introduced to their friend Hank everyone stood looking at the well laden watercraft and searching for signs of any dangerous sea creatures.

"I can't believe you didn't scare up a few of them sea bats, maybe us catching and eating them all the time has thinned their ranks some." Hank said who appeared to be a 35-ish medium built looking man with a bandage around his leg. He asked Annie to borrow her Kayak paddle and then poked the sand and water around Hogan's boat so they could unload some gear.

"Hank has developed quite a well deserved aversion to those venomous things. We found him sick as dog about a week ago looking awful pitiful waving at us from the beach after being stung by one." Sam said.

"I think I must be allergic to them things, I thought I was going to die at first." Hank said while unwrapping the bandage to show them an angry red sore on his calf.

"It looks better today; that hole in his leg actually turned sort of blue for awhile. Good thing Sam knew what to do for it." Lori said not having that crucial medical skill in her repertoire to help the man.

"Hogan, heed some advice if you even think about sprinting down this beach and going for a swim be sure to slow down and start shuffling as soon as your feet hit the water." Sam said and noted the confusion his guests had to that statement.

"The best way to make sure stingrays steer clear of your feet is to slide your feet along the sand instead of taking big steps. The shuffling sends vibrations that scare away stingrays in the immediate vicinity, thus you won't accidentally step on one. The idea is to try to push the sand forward and cause a disturbance that displaces the stingray without you stepping on it. If you step on it, you're in bad trouble, when you say oh hell and try to get away — that's when they get the barb in you." Sam said warningly.

"Not all rays are bad though; there are many types of rays in Florida waters. Most of them can't cause you any kind of harm. The Sting Ray can cause a painful wound. They lay on the sandy bottom partially covered with sand. Sometimes only their eyes are poking out of the sand. Sting Rays have a sharp bony barb at the base of their tails. If you step on the animal, it reacts by lashing its tail at your foot. The barb does have venom and it causes what I hear a very painful wound which can easily produce a nasty infection." Lori said as Sam and Annie stared at the ocean bottom.

"I've seen grown men break down and cry, they hurt so much. I thought I was going to also if I hadn't gotten so nauseous while having such a hard time breathing on top of the pain to get around to it though. If one those devilish things get you good, it will put you down for the count let me tell you. But the good news is that the additional side effects don't last very long except when you consider being in excruciating pain that peaks in 1-2 hours. You really got to be careful around them creatures because although not aggressive they are not terribly shy and will allow you to approach quite closely before fleeing." Hank said reaffixing his bandage.

"Haven't you ever seen one of those signs in touristy parts of Florida that warn you about those things? I call the little beach dance I do the Tampa Bay shuffle; most folks refer to it just doing the stingray shuffle. The best way to avoid Sting Rays is to shuffle your feet when you are walking in the water." Sam said.

"Sting rays around here are particularly common this month, Hogan, and it is not unusual to see a dozen or more swimming away if you are the first person in the water." Lori warned.

"Ok, here are a couple of the unwritten rules around here. Stingrays travel in schools and they like to come up to shore between 11 a.m. and 3 p.m., which also seems to be when most people think of coming to the beach. We haven't had too many boats come by but that's when you need to be out of the water and watching for boaters. We haven't had anybody playing pirate around here we know of but you can never tell. Did you and Annie have anybody give you all any trouble heading over here?" Sam asked.

"No, we wave to other people we see out on the water and they wave back but we usually keep our distance if we can. Now Atlanta on the other hand sounded like the fourth of July there for awhile but we were mostly hiding out in the woods on the river so I cant tell you exactly what's going on there." Hogan said thinking that the echoes of gunfire were an everyday occurrence back in the city.

"We try not to have any fires going during those times but we have been building one late afternoons to help start getting rid of the mosquitoes as well as for safety's sake when we are going in the water. You all need to remember this bit of advice also. If you are stung by a ray, the best remedy is to soak the affected area in a bucket of water. You want to get that water as hot as you can without burning your foot. You need to do this for about an hour and a half. What happens is, the heat will cause immediate pain relief by starting to neutralize the poison. We keep us a bucket of hot water on the campfire kind of like most snack bars and lifeguard stations have hot water and buckets ready for stingray incidents. Keep in mind also, if you get stung you should, while still in the water, irrigate the wound with sea water; that helps some with the pain and infection also." Sam said seriously but still smiling at the sight at of his old friend and the new acquaintance he had brought.

"All good to know stuff eh, Annie?" Hogan said looking over at Annie who was taking all the wise advice in.

"So Hogan you saw our Tetra Pod and decided to pay us a visit." Lori said not believing that after everything that had occurred that was such bad luck for them all had allowed for such a great reunion.

"You were lucky to have seen that boat and the fact that we were still in camp. I usually try to camouflage that Tetra Pod better but me and Lori were going to drag it down to the clearing and try using it for a deer blind. There is a clearing and a small fresh water lake back about a ¼ mile from here." Sam said before explaining to Hogan he had a duck blind for the boat that could do double duty as a deer hide.

"I ain't worth much for helping out pushing or pulling right now." Hank said referring to his injured leg.

ATV Off road version shown. (Sam's version has only two wheels and is meant to be pulled by a vehicle on a paved road."

"I smelled you cooking, is there anything you need to tend to?" Annie asked wondering if they had forgotten about their campfire.

"Oh yea we got to be getting back to that. What you were smelling coming from the cook fire was us making flat bread. Come on and join us for supper we got plenty, that is if you like scallops." Sam said with a wry smile.

"I love scallops!" Annie said brightly ready for a wonderful treat.

"He is funning with you Annie, what we are actually having is sting ray. Do they taste like scallops? You bet, Stingray and their relatives do make good eating and I can cook one all sorts of ways. I guess you have heard the myths about some Florida restaurants using a cookie cutter on a ray and serving them as scallops? I always doubted that to be true because the procurement of any kind of stingray "scallops" in restaurant quantity would cost more than buying the real thing. But I make a cookie cutter of sorts by sharpening the edge of a two-inch iron pipe with a file. When I hammer it though the wing of a ray, the makeshift cutter produces a neat plug of meat which after the skin is sliced away it makes a passable scallop." Hank said being a connoisseur of such.

"I wouldn't even know how to begin cleaning one." Hogan said intrigued.

"Ain`t much to it, if you can filet a flounder you can fillet a stingray. The only difference being between the two is that rays have cartilage in place of bones. I got two over there that I haven't got around to cleaning yet, come on and I will show you how to do it."

First Hank placed the small ray lying flat on the split log he was using as a cleaning table. Next he showed Hogan and Annie how to poke with your finger to find the line where the tender wing joins the hard back. Then using a sharp fish filleting knife, he sliced downward along the line from front to back, just deep enough to reach the cartilage.

Next he showed them that you then turn the knife blade flat and work it along the top of the cartilage out toward the wingtip—just like separating the fillet from the bones of a typical fish.

"Well now I know what to do with one. I never thought about them being edible before. Next time I crank up a stingray instead of my intended catch I won't cuss it and I will eat it instead." Hogan said.

"I have heard some folk's debate at a dockside bar whether or not something was a real scallop or not so I heard about that ray thing before but had forgotten about that. So you think that's not true huh? Dang look at the size of that Sting ray Hogan." Annie said pointing at one that was about two and a half feet in size.

"Oh they get bigger than that. With one this size you simply cut off the wing, place it in a pot, and simmer it for about 30 minutes. Unless you have a very big pot in your gear, you'll probably need to cut the wing in halves. Once you get them good and parboiled, the skin comes off rather easily. It also makes it easier to scrape the meat away from the cartilage. Now something I like to do in some of my cooking is kill two birds with one stone by adding spices or other flavorings to the water in which I parboil the wing. Once you flavor that water up you can refer to it as bouillon or broth depending on what you want to use it for." Hank said giving them cooking instructions.

"Oh he has lots of good recipes and we make do all right. Hank is a great cook; I just wish we had access to some things he needs to do it right. Hogan, we need to find us some chickens for eggs. He has a fried scallop recipe I have been dying to try." Lori said before letting Hank recite it to them.

MOCK SCALLOPS

2 stingray wings, filleted, skinned, cubed
2 eggs beaten
1 cup plain bread crumbs (more if needed)
Salt and pepper
Garlic powder

Take your cubes from the thickest portion of the wing as these are best for this recipes treatment, although I must say the thinner parts are good too. Sprinkle cubes lightly or to taste with salt, pepper and garlic powder. Dip cubes in beaten egg, then in bread crumbs. Fry at about 350 degrees until golden brown.

"Problem is we are getting light on garlic powder and we don't have any cooking oil." Hank said.

"I got a bit of both oil and garlic powder. Where we can find a chicken I haven't a clue but I would trade most anything for some." Hogan said.

"I have some garlic cloves I am going to need to plant before too long." Annie said.

"Ah, you have hidden treasure? I think you have been holding out on me, Annie!" Hogan joked but overjoyed with the news.

"No to be honest I just now thought about those cloves and us needing to plant them." Annie said thinking they were indeed a treasure now and the only source of replenishable seasoning and medicine that they had.

"Plant them here; we got plenty of fish gut fertilizer and seaweed to make them grow." Lori suggested.

"We can do that. I have some herb seeds also to plant!" Annie said excited that she could make such a great contribution to the group's diets and wellbeing. Spices equal happiness particularly when you are limited to consuming only certain things for awhile. Without them, food boredom can rapidly set in.

"After we get us a bite to eat you can help us move the Tetra Pod back to the field by the lake. There are alligators in that lake by the way but you can kayak there, if you use good sense. I have never seen it done in an inflatable before though." Hank said.

"It's pretty much the same being around gators in an inflatable as it is in a hard body kayak. If you ever have to borrow mine this fact might make you feel a little safer using it. If you are kayaking in an inflatable kayak most of the material components in these type kayaks are designed to keep you afloat even if the hull of your boat is punctured. For example, even the smallest Sea Eagle 330 inflatable kayak has three separate air chambers for the floor and each side of the kayak." Annie said which got everyone talking about kayaking around gators. Here are a few things they agreed on. Everyone was up for a little alligator poaching to reduce the threat and vary the cook pot.

Things to Remember When Paddling Near Alligators.

They mostly agreed that despite their stealth and cunning, alligators are not a creature to be feared; instead they should be treated with respect.

Hogan said he had no problem respecting them but would rather shoot them on sight if they were going to be using the lake access a lot.

Pretty much everyone understood attacks on kayaks and canoes are rare, but paddlers should remain watchful and cautious around these animals and when one is spotted it should be given it a respectful distance.

When paddling it's important to remember that, like sharks, alligators are most active at dusk and dawn. During the day they like to hang out near shore amid thick plant growth and can often be spotted basking onshore just around bends in creeks and rivers. Paddlers should avoid paddling too close to the shore, especially when negotiating turns. Never block an alligator's escape route to the water.

Now although a gator will slip off a bank on your approach and might be somewhere underneath you and may even follow you a little, stay calm and know that it will not "thump" you from underneath or lunge out of the water at you. Keep paddling, be wary, and if you are a little spooked a group of kayakers familiar with alligators advise that you bang your paddle on your kayak a few times to intimidate it. Some believe this may sound like wounded prey thrashing about in the mud possibly peaking its interest. Now I would try use my survival whistle because their hearing is sensitive. Since this isn't a scientifically tested method, distance is the safest recourse. Of course if these methods fail and the vessel is attacked, I agree try to remain calm and use the paddle for defense. Strike hard and get away fast.

"Here is a tidbit that I heard that might help you decide how close to get to an alligator. Someone once told me that a 7-foot alligator can kill an adult, a 9-footer can eat them and all alligators no matter how small will leave you with a nasty bite that you'll remember for the rest of your days.

For me, distance depends on the size of the 'gator. My personal rule goes like this - stay 4 feet away for every one-foot of length of the gator, with a minimum of 10 feet. So 5-foot alligators get 20 feet of room. A 10-footer gets 40 feet. You can make up whatever you feel comfortable with. If you see one go under going in one direction, go round in the opposite direction: chances are he will keep going in the direction he was headed. Traveling in groups helps also.

If you see young gators, do not approach them. Even though a 12 inch gator may look very cute, an 8 foot mother nearby will not like you for a babysitter.

An alligator with a hissing, open mouth is issuing a clear warning to back off. Never approach an alligator nest or baby alligators because the mother will aggressively defend her young.

There were other suggestions for avoiding the prehistoric reptiles but everyone knew to be on their guard for them and the subject changed.

"Let me show you my latest project, Hogan. Hank made me think of it because even though he was an experienced "wade" fisherman that shuffled his feet when moving forwards in the water, the stingray that had got him was one he had accidentally stepped backwards on." Sam advised explaining how the accident had occurred to the seasoned fisherman.

Hogan had seen anglers before that practiced a type of fishing that involved wading out from shore into waist-deep water to get near a shelf or drop-off, so he was familiar with the kind of fishing Sam was talking about.

"I started studying about how to maybe get out of the water to fish and maybe build me something on the bottom to stand on at low tide and come up with what I think is a great idea. Now this winter the water is going to be very cold due to the season. So standing on something makes sense and gets you out of the cold water. I have a ladder and homemade anchoring structures for a fishing platform that I am trying out. There are a few other reasons that a ladder in the water is good, like sight fishing and making it easier to cast. Sam had tied a floatation device to his ladder to help locate it if it fell over.

"Now that looks like a pretty unique way to fish. I would rather float on my boat though and watch you perch on that thing." Hogan said speculating he didn't much like the idea of fishing from a partially submerged ladder.

"The fishing out there is excellent, let me tell you. There is an unusual drop off right there that narrows towards the bend the fish and crabs congregate at. If you go out at low tide, you barely get your feet wet. Come on, I will show it to you while we still have plenty of sunlight to see down into the water!" Sam said.

"Ah hell here we go. So to move around in this lagoon of yours I got to shuffle." Hogan said and proceeded to exaggeratedly but safely doing the dance as his friend had recommended and stomped his feet and splashed the water a time or two to make noise upon entering so that the rays would swim away even if they couldn't see him. Hogan and Sam then shuffled along in the sandy bottom watching flitting shapes and sand sprays coming from departing sting rays as they proceeded towards Sam's fishing tower contraption.

"I still ain't liking this!" Hogan said clutching the Super Stick push pole with the flounder gig on the end of it that Sam had handed him as a confidence builder to step out into the ocean that far after all the dire warnings of today.

"Once you do it a time or two, walking out here becomes just instinctive and you care less about the rays. If you were hungry you could have tried to poke one of those things. They grill up pretty good just searing them on each side on a piece of corrugated tin we place over the coals of a fire." Sam said.

"Are you going to stay with us here, Hogan?" Sam asked.

"That's going to depend on what other nutty things you ask me to do!" Hogan said with a laugh as both men reached the ladder and climbed up for a look see into this alleged seafood honey hole.

"We have a lot to adapt to before this story is done. Walking that minefield of sting rays is but one of many things we must learn to overcome and persevere at in order to survive." Sam said as he looked over his shoulder and saw Lori giving Annie a hiking staff on the beach and some last minute instruction before they gave it a go.

THE END

Closing Thoughts

"The fears that burn in your mind today should not blind you to the speculations of tomorrow, but instead they should alert you to their presence by the smoke you see on the horizon of today." December 13, 2016 Ron Foster in regards to clouded judgments.

"Live by your first instinct and die by your last." Author unknown

Valuable Supporters And Vendors

RELi3ON®

Charlie Messina
Regional Sales Director
Toll Free: +1.844.385.9840
Office: +1.803.547.7288
Mobile: +1.704.634.4845
Cmessina@RELiONbattery.com

People. Power. Progress www.RELIONbattery.com

COUPON CODE

Bug Out Boat
Get a Free Battery Charger with purchase!
A truly exceptional savings and value for my readers and support for the Prepper Community

ADVENTURE TO GO!
Now Just $349
America's Most Popular Inflatable Kayak
Packs in a bag
FREE Ground Shipping to 48 Contiguous US
Easy to Carry, Easy to Set Up, Easy to Paddle,
Easy to Store, Could You Ask for More?
Our Sea Eagle 370 inflatable kayak provides instant adventure to go! This large 12' 6" inflatable kayak packs to the size of a small duffel bag, inflates in less than 8 minutes and can be used almost anywhere there is water. Paddle wild rivers, remote ponds, scenic lakes... even ocean surf! The Sea Eagle 370 weighs just 32 lbs., holds up to 650 lbs. of people & gear. This great inflatable kayak features 2 deluxe kayak seats with deluxe valves, 2 skegs for better tracking, 5 deluxe air valves, drain valve, rigid I-beam floor, spray skirts & carry handles.
SPECIAL PACKAGE PRICE - Our Sea Eagle 370 Pro Kayak Package includes: SE 370 kayak, 2 8' 4-Part Aluminum Paddles, 2 Super Comfortable Deluxe Kayak Seats, Foot Pump, Repair Kit and Convenient Nylon Shoulder Strap Carry Bag that holds it all.
NOW ONLY $349. with FREE SHIPPING!
6 month Trial Guarantee / 3 Year Warranty Against Defects.
Visit SeaEagle.com for more details
Call 1-800-748-8066 Mon-Fri, 9-5 EST
SE370
Join us on /SeaEagleBoats
SEA EAGLE.com
Dept AT017B,
19 N. Columbia St., Suite 1
Port Jefferson, NY 11777

Rugged "Roll Up"
10.6 Sport Runabout
The perfect ship to shore tender, dive boat, fishing boat or run about. With the rigid, inflatable keel and a 15 hp engine, you'll cut through water, wind & waves with ease.
Available with a high pressure inflatable floor or plastic floor boards.
• Measures 10'6" x 5'5"
• 90 lbs with high pressure inflatable floor
•124 with plastic floorboards
• 5 adults or 1200 lb load capacity
• 15hp gas engine capacity
• Deflates to 46"x24"x10" (hull)
SEAEAGLE.com
For Free Catalog Call 1-800-748-8066
19 N. Columbia St., Suite 1, Dept. PY116B
Port Jefferson, NY 11777
Join us on
/SeaEagleBoats
/SeaEagleBoats

Daiwa LUVIAS3000H Luvias Spinning Reel Features:

- Magsealed main shaft
- Zaion body
- Aluminum body cover
- Digigear system
- Aluminum ABS Spool
- Machined aluminum screw-in handle
- Protrusion free airbail
- Infinite anti-reverse
- Twist Buster II
- Deep aluminum spool
- Made in Japan

Valuable Supporters And Vendors

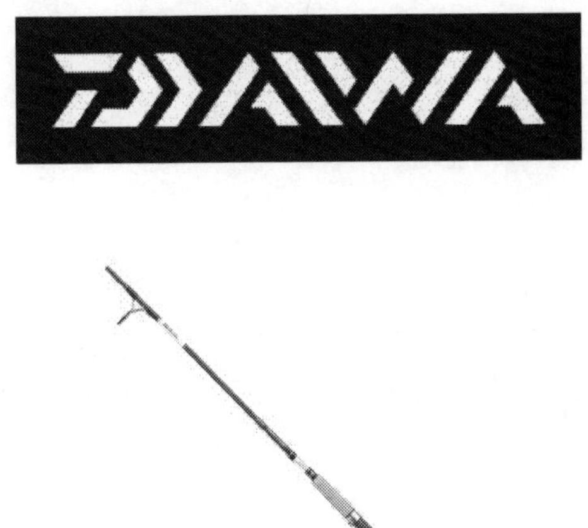

Providing enjoyment and positive feeling to fisherman for years.

Daiwa's evolution has always been associated with their state-of-the-art technology

Daiwa Harrier Inshore Spinning Rods are perfect for most inshore fishing applications. These rods are made with X45 Bias Graphite fiber construction - 45 degree bias construction prevents twisting of the blank for greater strength, sensitivity and hook setting power.

Daiwa Harrier Inshore Rods Features:

- Full natural cork handle
- Fuji-aluminum oxide guides
- Fuji DPS Reel seat
- 5 year limited warranty

Valuable Supporters And Vendors

"The Greatest Fish Catcher of All Time"

About Panther Martin

58 years of bringing in the big ones!

Panther Martin is known as one of the world's best spinning lures. It is the original inline spinner. The unique design of the Convex/Concave blade with the shaft going directly through the blade was first introduced in America by Panther Martin.

Panther Martin is known particularly for catching trout, but it is also proven through the years to be truly effective for salmon, steelhead, bass, pike, pickeral, muskie, crappie, panfish and many other species.

In its history over 104,000,000 Panther Martin lures have been sold. It is truly one of the world's great fishing lures.

What's New And Exciting

Valuable Supporters And Vendors

Bearded Banshee™

NEW Bearded Banshee™ is designed specifically for Smallmouth and Largemouth Bass. This bucktail spinner bait also features the Free Floating Sonic Arm to allow our convex/concave blade to swing freely and creates irresistible sonic vibrations that cause Smallmouth and Largemouth Bass to go into a feeding frenzy!

WeedRunner™

NEW WeedRunner™ is effective for both freshwater and saltwater fish. It is our first truly WeedLess Panther Martin® using our unique convex/concave Panther Martin® blade with a single hook embedded in a fluke/shad style tail. Particularly useful in saltwater flats or weed-infested lakes, this lure will catch many kinds of both freshwater and saltwater fish.

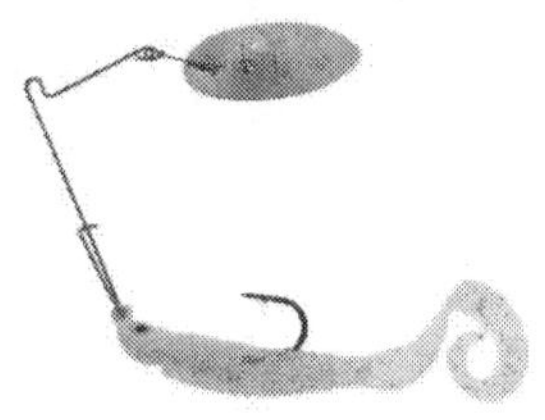

Valuable Supporters And Vendors

Sonic SizzleTail™

NEW Sonic SizzleTail™ is our first jighead style spinner. It works well in saltwater for Redfish, Sea Trout, Snook, Striped Bass and Flounder. It is also a very productive in freshwater for catching Bass, Walleye & Northern Pike. A unique feature of this lure is the Free Floating Sonic Arm that allows the blade to swim freely. The unique design of the Free Floating Sonic Arm creates irresistible vibrations that literally call the fish from afar!

Valuable Supporters And Vendors

With almost three decades of experience in semiconductor and solar energy research and development, PowerFilm has positioned itself as the leading global developer and manufacturer of thin-film solar products and modules. The company utilizes a unique and proprietary technology platform, enabling the production of low-cost solar modules on a high volume basis. And, we are proud to say that the manufacturing of our material and products is all done in the United States.

•

PowerFilm panels are ideal for bug out bags and other outdoor activities due to their being exceptionally portable, lightweight, durable and efficient. Their flexibility makes for a variety of possibilities in terms of how they can be set up, throw it on a tent, hang it from a tree, backpack or just roll it out in the ground.

Valuable Supporters And Vendors

THE TNW ASR

THE AERO SURVIVAL RIFLE

AVAILABLE IN 9MM, .40S&W, .45ACP, 10MM AND .357SIG
MULTI-CALIBER KITS AVAILABLE

The Aero Survival Rifle, famous for its removable barrel and easily convertible caliber changes, is a winner in home defense, backpacking, boating, and back country flying.

Valuable Supporters And Vendors

RECOMMENDED READING

This is my special personal recommendation and thank you for some good reading from a great writer. The truly delightful stories contained in this blog by the president of Sea Eagle reminded me of some of the finer moments and memories contained in the classic book "The Great Gatsby" How else would you describe someone that tells true stories of being raised around the famous Gabor sisters, New York socialite parties, boats and exceptionally great entrepreneurship?

Tangled Tales of An American Family
https://tangledtalesofanamericanfamily.com/

ABOUT

These are some stories about my family and myself. I call them tangled tales. They may not be completely correct because of my imperfect memory or because much time has passed since the events occurred or because I wish to protect the not so innocent. Copyright 2011.

I would like to mention that I periodically rewrite these articles, trying to eliminate typos, errors of fact or to add new information or material as it becomes available. As a matter of course, I regard nothing as finished.

Cecil Hoge

590 Mariner

#50299

The Mossberg® 590® Mariner Tactical Pump-Action Shotgun comes with a corrosion-resistant Marinecote finish, inside and out, to withstand the punishment of harsh saltwater environments. This is an ideal self-defense shotgun to have in a boat or yacht; as well as carrying in a vehicle that frequents humid coastal areas. The 590 Mariner also makes a practical, low-maintenance home defense shotgun and is one of the best firearms to carry while fishing or camping in bear country

Made in the USA
Columbia, SC
16 April 2018